STO

A fine
after t
item by
renewe
charges
www.st

0060263776

STING OF DEATH

Devoted wife and mother Linda Campion is found dead in her hall, sprawled on the marble floor, clutching a Catholic medallion of Saint Thérèse. An accidental tumble over the banisters? A suicidal plummet? Or is there an even more sinister explanation? As the police investigation begins to unearth family secrets, it becomes clear that all was not well in the household: Linda's husband Edmund — not long home from the war — has disappeared; and one of their guests has recently killed himself . . .

SHELLEY SMITH

STING OF DEATH

Complete and Unabridged

LINFORD
Leicester

First published in Great Britain

First Linford Edition
published 2018

A catalogue record for this book is available
from the British Library.

ISBN 978–1–4448–3637–0

Published by
F. A. Thorpe (Publishing)
Anstey, Leicestershire

Set by Words & Graphics Ltd.
Anstey, Leicestershire
Printed and bound in Great Britain by
T. J. International Ltd., Padstow, Cornwall

This book is printed on acid-free paper

PART ONE

1

She lay doubled over on the marble floor in the limp extravagant attitude of a ballerina's final curtsy, with her skirts spread about her, her flung-out arms very white and slender against the blue stuff and her hair like a sprawling blot of ink. One foot pointed elegantly from beneath the skirt.

Coming into the hall from the sunlight, Ivor did not see her till he was almost on her. It was shadowy in the well of the staircase, but he did not need to touch her; her attitude was unmistakable. Besides, he felt an understandable reluctance to contact that cold flesh.

The hall seemed very airless and dark to him. He thought desperately, I must get out of here, and turned away with his uneven step. His face in the spotted Venetian mirror was a greenish khaki. 'Christ, boy, you look sick!' he muttered dryly, and glanced nervously behind him, as if Linda were listening. Linda! He must not *think* about Linda.

There was a moment when it seemed he could walk out again as unobserved as he had entered and leave somebody else to discover the body, but the reluctant habit of responsibility was stronger than his momentary neurotic self-pity and he unhooked the old-fashioned wall telephone that hung in the hall.

'Dr. Wellesley?' he said. 'Will you come round to Hawkswood at once — before your surgery . . . ? No, it's not for me. It's urgent. There's been an accident. Mrs. Campion has been killed. Thank you,' he said, listening to the intent silence and then slowly replacing the earpiece on its hook. He was trembling.

The letters! Jesus God! I'll have to get them before they fall into anyone else's hands. But to get upstairs he would have to pass that still thing in the hall. The staircase spiraled dizzily before him with its elegant wrought-iron rails. Somewhere to the left he heard a door open and close. He turned to meet the steps as they were coming toward him.

4

The tall handsome old man broke into a genial smile as false as his teeth and squeezed the palm of his hands together: 'Ah — er — Campion, my boy! Back already, eh?'

'Sir, I must speak to you. Can we go into the library?'

'Well, well, well,' said the old man patronizingly, 'what's up? You're looking a bit green about the gills. Had one of your bad turns, eh? Care for a drink?'

'Mr. Marriot, there's no time to lose. It's about your daughter I wanted to see you. There's been an accident . . . I wish I wasn't the one who had to break it to you . . . She must have fallen over the banisters. I've sent for the doctor, though there's nothing he can do.'

'Where is she? I must go to her.'

'No,' said Ivor, gently pressing him back. The old man stared at him, and comprehension washed a ghastly shadow over his handsome ruddy face. '*Dead?*' he said. 'My little girl? My little Linda?' His eyes looked frightened. He pressed his hands together: 'I can't believe my little girl's left me . . . What will become of her

5

old father now?' he muttered, staring into the future with shaking lips.

Ivor turned his back and gazed out of the window to give the old boy time to pull himself together.

He recalled with a kind of anguish his last words to Linda, only a few hours ago; but his mind shrank from their implications.

There was the distant sound of a car drawing up, and Ivor hurriedly left the room.

'Bad business,' said Dr. Wellesley, greeting him tersely. 'Where is she?'

'There. Where she fell.'

'Ah!' said Dr. Wellesley, kneeling by the body and touching it with practiced hands. 'What happened?'

Ivor shrugged. 'Fell over the banisters, I suppose.'

'Did you see her fall?'

'Good God, no!' said Ivor violently. 'I just came in and saw her there.'

'Move the body at all?'

'I didn't even touch her, believe me.'

'It's the police who must believe you, not me.'

'The police?' said Ivor stupidly. 'Why the police?'

'Because there will have to be an inquest, to determine the cause of death.'

'Isn't that your job?' said Ivor sulkily.

Dr. Wellesley grunted and stood up.

'Well, I can't do any more until they come. They'll be here soon.'

'Did you tell them to come?' said Ivor in a high-pitched voice.

'Yes. That's my job,' said Dr. Wellesley coolly. 'I daresay that's them now.'

A tremor of indecision shook Ivor's frame, and then he said, 'All right,' and jerked himself quickly up the stairs and out of sight.

There were two policemen: a big sergeant with blank blue eyes that looked at nothing and saw everything, in a wooden face; and a slender dark inspector with dangerously sympathetic eyes and the long mobile mouth of an actor. As they worked they grunted a few questions from time to time at the little doctor.

'Fell over the banisters, eh?'

'It would appear so.'

'How long she been dead?'

7

'Speaking very roughly, about two hours.'

'You'd almost think, lying in the hall like this, she'd have been found before now, wouldn't you?'

'In the middle of the afternoon? You know what these country houses are: they'll have been busy, or out, or sleeping on their beds, or something. You'll see.'

'I daresay I shall,' said Inspector Trevor gloomily. 'Not a nice welcome to the district, I must say. I suppose she was the lady of the manor, so to speak. Can't see what she looked like in that position, but she seems to have been quite young. D'you know how old she was?'

'Twenty-eight, poor kid. Nice little thing she was, too. If you've finished, we'll remove the body.'

As they moved her, the sunlight gleamed on a fine silver chain that dangled from her clenched hand.

Campion came walking down the passage toward him with an anxious expression on his saturnine face.

'How are you feeling?' the doctor said.

'All right.'

'Good! The police want to have a few

words with you. You'll find them in the billiard room.'

The police saw a tall young man with a narrow disdainful face. His limp was more noticeable than usual as he crossed the room.

Inspector Trevor smiled encouragingly at him.

'I understand that you discovered the deceased lady, so I have just a few questions to ask you, and I think we'll start with your name.'

'Ivor Campion,' said Ivor in his high haughty voice.

'A relative?'

'Yes,' he agreed, stubbornly refusing to give more information than he was asked for.

'Do you live here?'

'I've been staying down here off and on for the last three months.'

'I see. Now would you describe to me your movements this afternoon? Say from about two o'clock.'

'Caught the two-thirty bus to Howces- ter. Had my hair cut and did a little shopping. Popped into a cinema for the big picture and caught the five-forty home. It was about five past six when I got in. The front door was open, as it always is in the summer. I walked toward the stairs, and then of course I saw her — poor dear!'

'How was she lying?'

'Just as she was when you saw her. I didn't touch her. I didn't need to.'

'You knew she was dead?'

'Yes.'

'I see. So you weren't surprised.'

'Surprised? I hardly understand you, I think,' he said haughtily. 'I was deeply shocked of course. It is a terrible thing to have happened. A most tragic accident.'

'And you knew at once she was dead.'

'I've seen death too often these last years not to recognize it.'

'Let us go back to the description of your movements, if you please, after you found her.'

'I telephoned the doctor.'

'And then?'

'Why, nothing! I was just — I just stayed where I was. And presently Mr. Marriot, Mrs. Campion's father, happened along, so I took him into the library and broke the bad news to him. He was very upset of course, and I stayed with him until I heard the doctor arrive.'

'I see. Now, if you'll just tell me how many people there are in the house and who they are, I won't need to trouble you anymore, at present.'

'Well, you already know of Linda and Mr. Marriot and myself. Then there are her children. Four of them, I believe, all about the same age and excruciatingly wild: Lionel, Oliver, Jane, and Charles; I think that's how they go. And old Nanny Potter, who keeps an eye on them, like a sleepy old tortoise; though it's Priss who does all the chivvying: Nanny Potter the shepherd and Priss the sheepdog. She's about twelve years old, I suppose: Linda's brother's child, Priscilla Marriot. Then there's Miss Sharpe, Linda's great-aunt; and the Hausers — or I should say, Ilse Hauser; her husband is dead.'

Here Ivor broke off and glanced quickly at the sergeant making notes in the corner: 'He'll remember all about that,' he said. But the sergeant's glance was unresponsive, as if he had never seen him before, as if they had never played darts together at The Soldier's Return. 'They were a couple of Austrian refugees. Werner owned a Catholic newspaper and suffered the usual Nazi persecution. Finally they managed to get over here, and Linda took them in,' Ivor resumed.

'Anyone else?'

'Not living here. Two village women come in the morning to do the rough work, but I'm afraid I don't know their names.'

'No husband?'

'Oh, yes! Edmund!' said Ivor with a queer expression. 'I'd actually forgotten about him for the moment. He'll have to be told, won't he? I suppose I'd better see to all that, as I'm his cousin. I'll telegraph to his London club.'

'Is he not expected home this evening?'

'No. He isn't living here just now.'

'Oh? Why not?'

'I should ask Campion about that, if I were you.'

The inspector raised his eyebrows politely, but otherwise ignored the snub.

'We'll just take a look at her room,' he said, 'if you wouldn't mind showing us where it is.'

Ivor went ahead of them quickly with a hasty compulsive glance at the vacant circle under the stairs. Ivor was explaining that Linda slept on the top floor to be near the children at night, when a lady came toward them in a floating negligee. She pulled the edges modestly together as they approached, and then impulsively drew close and put a hand confidently on Ivor's arm. With every movement emanated gusts of eau de cologne. Her hair was in loose waves to her shoulders. Her cheeks were flushed, her bright eyes moist, as if swimming with tears.

'My dear!' she said, with a charming foreign accent. 'I have heard! *Wie schrecklich!* A shocking tragedy! That poor child! Our little saint!'

Ivor said: 'This is Frau Hauser.'

'But of course,' she said quickly, smiling at Sergeant Drake, 'this good policeman and I are already knowing each other from when my poor Werner die. And now so soon, another tragedy. It is terrible!'

'Why are you up here, Ilse?' Ivor said curiously.

Frau Hauser permitted herself to express gracious surprise.

'What a question, Ivor, my dear! I come to take a bath.' She held up a large floral satin sponge-bag, bulging squarely. She turned for the first time the full luster of her eyes on to the inspector, and explained sweetly to the stranger: 'Here we are so many that who wishes to be clean must take his bath sharply at what time he may.'

'Since you are here, Mrs. — er — Hauser, perhaps you wouldn't mind telling us what else you did.'

She opened her chestnut-brown eyes very wide.

'But nothing, *Herr Kommissar*. I don't know what you mean.'

Ivor said: 'I think the *inspector* means that you won't have been all the afternoon taking a bath.'

'Oh, no! I am not so dirty!' She gave a little cooing laugh. 'All afternoon, since lunch, I am writing letters. I have much business letters to write since my poor

14

Werner is no more; I have no one to help me, and it is hard for me alone.' She sighed.

'I'm sure it is. One thing more, Mrs. Hauser. How did you know that Mrs. Campion was dead?'

'Oh, that poor Mr. Marriot, he tell me. He is terribly grieving. And I am always very *sympatisch* to him. So we cry a little together and then he go away to, what he call, walk it off.'

They separated, and the two policemen followed Ivor into Mrs. Campion's bedroom. Then they politely dismissed him and got down to work.

The room was untidy and smelled faintly of rich tobacco smoke. The pink chintz coverlet on the bed was creased. On the dressing table was a large framed photograph of a soldier with blunt pugnacious features. The photographer by luck or real ability had contrived to give him a rather subtle look of a scowling faun, which made him, if not handsome, at least distinctive. *Edmund, with love*, was written in the corner.

'Wonder what they were looking for,

and whether they found it.'

'Sir?'

'Somebody's had a good but inter-rupted rummage in here. Don't you see? Something fairly small is my guess that could be hidden in a handkerchief drawer or under a pile of jumpers or behind a row of books. But not between the books evidently, for none appear to have been taken out, so it must have a certain bulk.'

'How can you tell that none were taken out, sir?' asked Sergeant Drake.

'I can't. But it looks as if someone just ran a hand along the spines and pushed them to the back of the shelf.'

'Maybe the lady kept them at the back like that.'

At this suggestion the inspector's dark eyes smiled and he ran a finger along the irregular line of dust at the edge of the shelf which marked the place where they habitually rested. 'See?' he said. 'Whoever it was didn't notice that, or hadn't the time to work them back.'

Inspector Trevor tidily removed a twisted bronze hairpin from the window sill and bent to sniff at a little bowl of stock.

There was also on the window sill a pottery ashtray with half a dozen pins and one cigarette stub in it, a plasticine donkey very gingerly poised, a Sévres potpourri bowl, a rosewood box inlaid with mother of pearl, and sitting in the corner, a shabby old doll that had fallen over on its face in a posture horribly reminiscent of the dead woman. The rosewood box contained some tinselly trinkets. There was a crack down one side of the bottom. Trevor pushed and the false bottom sprang back to reveal the cavity beneath. But within were only a lot of receipted bills and canceled checks and cut-out cooking recipes and a few old letters. When the inspector tried to close it up again he found the catch had been broken, so that it did not completely close.

As they made their way downstairs, a voice said sharply: 'What are you doing here?' and they turned to see a fragile old lady, with a face of wind-carved hone, regarding them severely from eyes like coals.

'Good evening, ma'am,' said Inspector Trevor ingratiatingly.

She rapped her stick on the marble.

'What are you doing here? Clattering up and downstairs as if the place belonged to you! Is there to be no privacy any longer! Since this war people seem to have taken leave of their senses! Go away!' Her stick pointed to the door. 'Go along! Be off with you, I say!'

Inspector Trevor came up to her slowly like an animal trainer. His face was kind, his brown eyes gentle.

'Miss Sharpe?' he said. 'When did you last see Mrs. Campion?'

'What's that girl been up to now?'

'There's been an accident,' he began.

'I've warned her, I've warned her!' said the old lady with a mixture of triumph and contempt in her manner. 'Girl drives like a fool, but it's not a bit of use your coming to me for help.' She began to turn away with the careful footsteps of the aged, and then turned back to ask: 'Anybody hurt?'

'It was a fatal accident,' Trevor said gently. 'But it was not motoring. Your niece fell to her death.'

The old woman stood with her back to

them in silence for a long minute. Trevor took her arm and gently pushed her into a chair. She looked bewildered.

'It's the loss,' she said in a shaky old voice. 'The children . . . At my age one has got so used to the idea of death that it ceases to shock one, but when it's someone young, someone needed — ' Her voice broke. 'Of course, that man killed her,' she said.

'What man?'

She looked up at Trevor with something of her former expression.

'None of your business. I was thinking aloud. A privilege of the old.'

'Could you now answer my question? When did you last see Mrs. Campion?'

'At luncheon. Afterwards I went to my room. And I believe my niece went to hers. I know she asked Priscilla to look after the children because it was Nanny Potter's day out — as a rule she looks after them herself on those days. The German woman did the washing-up.'

'It was unusual, then, for your niece to retire to her room?'

'I've just said so.'

'Why did she, do you suppose?'

'I thought she looked tired. Rather white. I advised her to have a rest, and she said she would.'

'Did she seem herself otherwise? Not depressed, or worried, or unhappy?'

'She seemed herself. Who isn't depressed or worried or unhappy in these days? Now I'm tired of answering questions. Go away, my dear sir.' She closed her eyes decisively.

Ivor Campion was smiling cynically when he joined them outside.

'So you've been interviewed by Miss Sharpe, have you? What did you think of her?'

'She took it very well, I thought,' said Trevor moderately.

'Old bitch!' said Ivor. 'Wait till you know her better. What a life she led that poor girl! If Linda hadn't been a saint, she'd have throttled her.'

'Did she seem any different from usual today? Mrs. Campion, I mean, not Miss Sharpe of course.'

Ivor turned his head away and stared across the park.

'Here come the children. Poor little rats, they'll have to be told too . . . No, she didn't seem any different to me.'

'We'll have the husband's London address, if you please. Drake, make a note of it!'

The children were slanting away from the front of the house, toward the back. Trevor followed casually after. They were twittering shrilly together like birds. A ladder, like a bit of Freudian surrealism, leaned against the house and the children ducked underneath it with fingers crossed in a wish. A small dark-haired girl drew back suddenly against a taller girl's skirts. A boy darted forward and seized her by the hand to drag her through . . .

'Come *on!*' they heard him cry impatiently. 'You got to, silly!'

She said: 'No!' and pulled away.

An older boy pushed her from behind. She was encircled by their ominous goblin faces. Even Priss didn't understand. In despair the small girl flung herself on the ground and bellowed till her face was as red as a dahlia. Priscilla said wearily:

'There! You've made her cry again. You are naughty boys!' and picked her up laboriously in her skinny little arms. They disappeared inside.

'Odd little animals!' commented Ivor vaguely.

'What's the ladder for?' asked Trevor, more interested in getting the lay of the land than in the little girl's nerve storms.

'Cleaning the gutters of old bird nests and rubbish before the bad weather comes. I'm getting quite nimble with my foot,' he said conceitedly.

'Where did you lose it?'

'When I was a P.O.W. in Italy. It went gangrenous with frostbite on the Long March. When we arrived in Germany they had to take it off. But of course I didn't get a new foot till I got back home, the week before V-E Day.'

As they drove away Inspector Trevor looked back at the shabby Palladian façade and said thoughtfully:

'This Werner Hauser. I gather he died fairly recently by what the merry widow said. Was it an accident?'

'Suicide, sir. It happened less than a

22

month ago. He was missing three days before we found him in one of the attics that used to be a servant's bedroom — when they had servants. He puts us off the track, you see, sir, because he borrowed the car and drove off in it. Then some four miles from here, we figure he got out, left the car there, and walked back to Hawkswood, entered the house unseen, and crept up into the attic to die alone. Sad, really.'

'No question of anything but suicide?'

'No, sir. An overdose: one of the barbiturates.'

'Any suggestion why he should have killed himself come out at the inquest?'

'Oh, well, sir, it was pretty plain really. All that persecution does send them off their rockers a bit, don't you think?'

'Were they persecuted here?'

Sergeant Drake looked shocked.

'Oh, no, sir. But he'd been in one of these here concentration camps, it came out.'

'And so just when his enemies were beaten, he elects to kill himself. It seems an inopportune moment to me. What did the merry widow say?'

'Very cut up, sir, very tearful.' He met the inspector's eye. 'You can't ever tell with some women though, can you? I mean, it may have been genuine enough and she may have been just putting on an act this afternoon.'

'It's quite a possibility. But there was no 'act' about the eau de cologne she'd been swilling. I bet she's one of those quiet, helpless little tipplers who privately soak it up like a sponge . . . '

'It would be nice to know what she was really up to while she was supposed to be taking a bath, too. Wouldn't it? Did you feel the pipes? They were stone cold.'

'Yes, the lady was lying, I'm afraid. Why, I wonder?'

2

'Can I pour you a cup, Mrs. Potter?' said Mrs. Hacker civilly, reaching down from the dresser a blue cup and a white one with a pink rim and setting them in fawn and gold saucers because no matching china was left.

'I won't say no,' said Nanny Potter in her slow comfortable voice that sounded like a fat old family cat talking, and with a cat's comfortable wisdom, too. 'Cut yourself a nice slice of bread and dripping.'

'Couldn't touch a thing,' declared Mrs. Hacker, rolling the sleeves of her emerald 'woollie' up her stout red arms. 'It's quite put me off; upsets always fly straight to me stomach. And what it must have been like for you, Mrs. Potter, I shudder to contemplate; I do really. You having been with the family so long, it must feel like losing one of your own. And to think it might have been you who found her!'

'Little pitchers!' remarked Nanny Potter inconsequentially, stirring her tea. Without turning her head she said: 'Don't hang about in the doorway, ducky. Either come in or go out.'

'Can I have some bread and dripping, Nanny?'

Oliver was a little thin boy of six with pale sandy hair and a small nervous face beneath a lofty brow.

'Poor little mite!' said Mrs. Hacker in the heartfelt tones of Lady Isobel of East Lynne, slapping dripping lavishly on the loaf. 'Do they *know?*' she asked Nanny Potter in a stagey whisper.

'Say thank you, Oliver. And then run along outside.'

'Thank you, Mrs. Hacker,' he said politely. 'I want to get my horse, Nanny . . . Please,' he added like a devout Amen. He scampered off and paused outside the door to hear Mrs. Hacker say: 'Whatever are you going to tell them?'

'We've told them she's gone away. Though mind you, I think Lionel ought to be told, him being the eldest. Still, we'll leave that for his father to decide.'

'When I think of those little motherless mites it makes my heart bleed,' said Mrs. Hacker impassioned, pressing the loaf to her breast as if to staunch the flow and absently cutting herself a thick slice, for properly to relish a tragedy one must keep up one's strength. 'Just a corner, Mrs. Potter. Do. To oblige me,' she urged. 'You must keep up your strength. Now more than ever. Who have those kiddies got but you, when all's said and done?'

'They have their father.'

'But he's more like a stranger, isn't he?'

'He's not to blame for that.'

'No, indeed,' said Mrs. Hacker agreeably. 'Another cup, Mrs. Potter? I suppose he'll be down sometime today?'

'That I am not in a position to say.'

'It'll be a blow to him, I make no doubt. I do wonder how ever it happened. Poor madam! Such a sweet young lady as she was. There'll be more than one that'll miss her that I know.' She looked at Nanny sideways out of her round brown eye like a bird.

'Oh, as to that . . . ' said Nanny ambiguously.

'He was the one that found her, wasn't he? Ts, ts! What a turn it must of give him. Fancy, two deaths in less than a month! It makes your flesh creep, don't it? There'll be more bad luck before this lot is through, you mark my words. Oliver!' she cried sharply, her eye caught by a movement behind the door. 'You come on out from there! Well, whoever would have thought he'd be so sly?' she said with an indignant flush, rolling her sleeves nervously up and down. 'I declare, your Nanny ought to give you a good hiding.'

'Nanny doesn't hide us ever,' Oliver said haughtily.

'Run and play, then.'

The little boy skipped airily away.

'Would you believe it? Little monkey!' exclaimed Mrs. Hacker. 'Aren't they sharp? I shouldn't wonder he didn't take it in, for all that.'

'All children are inquisitive. Something is up; but I should know soon enough if they had found out the truth. Priscilla has been told of course, but she's a very reliable little girl. The only one I've been worried about is Jane. Priscilla says she was very difficult yesterday, and she woke up in the night screaming. Some nightmare about a horrible man, she said. I gave her a little dose. All this psychology I don't believe in: an upset tummy mostly, believe me.'

'Miss Priscilla says she's mislaid her bicycle. I told her it was lucky her head was screwed on tight so she couldn't lose that. Of course being an orphan herself, she'll be able to sympathize with those mites. She must be a great help to you; four kiddies to look after at your age can't be much joke.'

'I'm used to children,' said Nanny Potter quietly. 'I was nursemaid to Mr. Edmund's mother when I was fourteen and I'll be content to end my days looking after her grandchildren.'

'That's the spirit, Mrs. Potter dear,' said Mrs. Hacker in a conciliating tone, rattling the ashes out of the boiler. 'Mr. Edmund'll be bound to be down for the inquest, won't he? Tomorrow did you say it was?'

★ ★ ★

'Exhibit A,' said Dr. Wellesley cheerily, handing Inspector Trevor a fine silver chain from which hung a small medallion. 'Worn round the deceased's neck as a rule, but in this instance I found it in her hand, her left hand. I'll tell you about that in a minute.'

Trevor turned it over in his fingers. It was not a locket or a pendant. It was an oval of silver about the size of a shilling and on one surface was enameled in blue a representation of a girl's head in profile with a rayed halo behind it. The fine chain dangled between his fingers like threads of gossamer in the sunlight. It was broken: the links close to the fastening had been violently wrenched apart. Round the edge of the medallion was written minutely: *The Little Flower of Jesus, St. Thérèse of Lisieux.*

'Ever heard of cadaveric spasm?' asked the doctor.

'You mean a sort of rigor mortis, only simultaneous with death. At the moment of death the hand contracts and fixes like that. The drowning man literally clutches at a straw. Isn't that it?'

'Yes. That is how Mrs. Campion, deceased, clutched that trinket. You can see where the chain was torn away. The skin at the back of the neck is considerably abraded. Look!' He pushed the heavy black hair away from the slender neck cinctured with a thin violet line.

'Could she have done that in cadaveric spasm?'

'She could,' the little doctor conceded. 'But she didn't, you know.' He pointed to the violet mark on the dead girl's neck. 'That was done after she was dead, for some reason. Ye-es,' he went on pensively, 'she died some two or three hours before I saw her.'

'Making it roughly some time between quarter-past three and quarter-past four? That's not possible, surely? She couldn't have lain in the hall for nearly three hours. Someone would have been bound to see her.'

'Oh, yes,' agreed the doctor. 'She can't have lain in the hall, as you say. That brings us to Exhibit B.' He picked up a small silky garment of a fancy mesh. He shook out the skimpy little vest and held it up by its thin ribbon straps. 'See there, a little brownish smear? Blood. There's nothing to show externally in the way of a wound, but that little spot of blood gave me a hint of what to look for. A little puncture under the left breast. The weapon penetrated the cage of the ribs and perforated the heart. Death must have been instantaneous. Moreover, she was lying on her back when she was killed or she fell on her back as she died, and she remained in that position for some not inconsiderable time. The condition of the blood vessels internally and on the buttocks and back, compressed by their position, show the characteristic changes we call *hypostasis*. The weapon was withdrawn from the heart, and later the body was dropped down the well of the stairs. That's about all I can tell you,' said Dr. Wellesley with assumed nonchalance.

'Quite enough, too, thank you. What a horribly unsavory affair. Beastly cold-blooded! The idea was to make it look like an accident, of course. That practically rules out suicide, manslaughter, and homicide, I'm afraid, and leaves us with a singularly brutal murder.'

★ ★ ★

Contrary to Nanny Potter's expectations, and everyone else's, Edmund Campion was not at the inquest — for the simple reason that he had not yet been found. When there was no reply to Ivor's telegram and even the last train of the day did not bring him in, Ivor phoned The Bath Club. The porter said Mr. Campion had not been in to collect his wire; he had gone away and left no forwarding address. Odd, said everybody; very rum! Edmund could hardly have chosen a more awkward moment, both for himself and the family, to disappear.

At the inquest nothing was made of it of course. The whole affair was handled very deftly and tactfully. But all the tact in the world could not smooth over the only one verdict which could possibly be brought in (and the jury accordingly did so): 'Willful murder by some person or persons unknown.'

The police work then began in earnest. To follow every step would be as tedious as it was for them, but some of the conversations were not without interest. Mrs. Hauser, for instance, still stuck to it that she had been in her room all the afternoon 'writing business letters.' (As might be expected, not one of them had a checkable alibi now that the germane time was between three and four.) Mrs. Hauser said she had been in her room *from* three o'clock approximately (as though that was any help!), for it had taken her the best part of an hour to clear and wash up after the midday meal. There had been no one to help her.

'I do it all alone,' she said grandly. 'Me. I make nothing of it, you understand; though some peoples think it is terrible thing that I, Ilse von Bergen that was, must do such things. In my country, it would be impossible. But me, I am very proud, and rather I do that than to live on charity which for me is quite dreadful. Also it pleases me very much to help this

34

poor girl, Linda, who like all your English women is not at all clever at making a *ménage*. So I must always be showing her how it should be done.'

'Was anyone with you, or near you, in the kitchen?'

'Ah, you are waiting to see if I speak the truth,' she said with a merry laugh. 'Yes, this old nurse is in the kitchen making ready the tea for the children because she is going out, so she leaves it for them prepared and that child Priscilla later will give it to them and for no one is it a trouble.'

'I see. So till three, approximately, you have a witness to your whereabouts; after that time we have only your word for what you were doing and where you were.'

'But of course,' she said ingenuously, opening wide her reddish-brown eyes.

'Did you hear any disturbance, anything unusual, during the afternoon?'

Ilse shook her head.

'My room is quite at the end of the corridor on the second floor. I could not hear if anyone comes to attack that poor girl.'

35

'Was the front door open all afternoon, do you know or not?'

'I do not *know* that it was open that day, but it was always kept open except when the weather is too cold.'

'You think it quite feasible for a person to enter the house and get upstairs without being seen?'

'But, yes; my dear sir. Of course.' She looked at him seriously, large-eyed. 'Is that not just what my poor Werner has done?'

'I understand that your husband committed suicide, Mrs. Hauser. And quite recently.'

'It is so. Life becomes too much for him.'

'Ts, ts, how sad!' commented Trevor, looking at her sympathetically. 'And just when the war had ended and things might be about to improve for him — for you both. Had he had bad news? Something of that sort?'

Ilse glanced down at her soft white hands folded in her lap, so that her dark red hair fell prettily round her face.

'For him it was bad news, because he has no longer the courage for life. And in

36

this terrible world one must have very, very much courage, I think. But when Werner is in Dachau they take away all his courage — ' her voice was quite expressionless — 'and he never find it again. So when Linda tells us we should go now, he is much afraid. He thinks nowhere there is to go now for people like us, nowhere where he can have peace, except he goes home to his father. And I think that because he is homeless God will not turn him away.' She put her handkerchief to her eyes. Then she sighed and stared at him sadly, intensely.

Trevor could feel himself blushing beneath the insistence of that dovelike dewy gaze. He had the impression that she was willing him to do or to say something.

'How long have you been here, Mrs. Hauser?'

'Oh, two years. We were living in London, and then our rooms became bombed, and so, one thing and another,' she shrugged expressively, 'we came here.'

'And here you would have been content to stay?'

'Till we can go to America, yes.'

'Only Mrs. Campion suggested your leaving before that, eh?'

'Not suggested. Insisted,' said Ilse, with a look of sour triumph. 'At once. A week's notice, you understand, like defaulting servants.' The sudden bitterness in her dulcet voice was shocking.

Trevor wondered who had given her that phrase — 'defaulting servants' — but he merely asked, 'Why?'

Ilse's mouth twisted sardonically.

'It is quite simple, you see. Her husband was come home from the war and she wished to be alone with him, so we must 'clear out'.'

'Like that!'

'More or less. For my part, I care not at all. Also, I am very proud; a von Bergen, you understand. But Werner can take no more, his spirit is too tired. Linda cannot understand this, the English have not suffered as we have; it is very bitter for us to have no fatherland any more, no home, no hope. And so Werner preferred to die than to struggle longer. That is all.' She gave a beautiful shrug of resignation.

'This must be very painful to you, Mrs. Hauser; but it is a fact, isn't it, that your husband left no message behind him?'

Frau Hauser inclined her head.

Trevor said: 'Then why are you so sure that that is why he killed himself?'

She gave a sad little laugh.

'Ah, my dear friend, do you imagine I have no experience of it before? Often my poor man has told me he will kill himself. It is what you call an old story, you may believe me. Only this time he is quite quite meaning it; and we cannot find him. We look and look; in the park, in the fields, in the road and the river. We do not think to look in the house all over. We think he must be near where he has left the car. But, you see, it was not so, and so this time he is quite dead before we find him.'

'No enemies you know of?'

She gave him a quick startled look.

'Enemies,' she repeated slowly. He could almost see her thoughts flying this way and that, confusedly. 'I do not ask myself such a question before, but it is impossible that a man in his position

39

should not have enemies — a foreigner, penniless, in a country at war with the country of his birth. Yes, it may be that Werner had many enemies.'

'And so perhaps he had some other reason than the one you have thought of for killing himself? Or perhaps, after all, he did not kill himself?'

Inexplicably Frau Hauser went scarlet.

'That is what you think? That is why you ask me all these questions about him?'

'My dear madam, it is not what I *think*, it is merely an idea put forth almost at random. I simply wondered if there might not be some connection between the one death and the other. Therefore if one was murder, so might the other be.'

'It is not so, Mr. Trevor. You must believe me that it is not so.'

'Just an idle speculation, Mrs. Hauser. Please do not distress yourself.'

★ ★ ★

Miss Sharpe had a fire in her room, though the weather was still warm, almost sultry indeed . . . an Indian summer. She sat very upright in the winged chair, her white hair brushed in a pompadour. Watching them advance without turning her head made her face appear more eagle-like than ever. She said with a dangerous sweetness, a kind of sugary acidity:

'Well, young man, what is it this time?'

'A few questions . . . '

'Ah, I am to tell you who the perpetrator of the crime is, I suppose? You want to know how you should run your business, eh? Why should you expect me to do your work for you?'

'Am I to understand that you are indifferent to the abrupt and cruel death of your great-niece?' the inspector said coldly.

'Ask me the right question and you'll get the right answer.' Her thin old hands stroked her skirt with pleasure at this gnomic retort.

'Tell me what you were doing, Miss Sharpe, on the afternoon your niece was killed.'

She said sharply: 'I told you that the

other day: I was *here*. I rest every afternoon. At my age one does not sleep after two or three in the morning. That afternoon, like every other, I rested.'

'Did you sleep?' he asked.

'I daresay I indulged in a little nap from time to time,' the old lady admitted, raising her eyebrows quizzically.

'Yet from your room you might have heard her fall.' She made no reply to this indirect question. 'Were you surprised to learn that your niece had been murdered?'

'Don't waste my time asking damned silly questions!' she said irritably.

'Why silly? From a remark you made to me the other afternoon it seemed as if you expected it. You said, you may remember, that *that man had killed her*. Evidently you anticipated something of the sort. You must have had some reason for jumping to the conclusion that it was murder. And I should like you to tell me whom you designated as *that man*.'

'Answer a fool according to his folly!' She sighed impatiently. 'Have you never heard of a person being driven to kill themselves? That was what I believed had happened to that poor child, Linda. Is it likely that I could know she had been murdered, my good man? Use your intelligence!'

'Driven to suicide by whom, if you please?'

'I believe you policemen have an old-fashioned dictum: *cherchez la femme*. Apply it, apply it! It surprises me that you people never think of reversing it — so much more applicable to women, I should have thought.'

'If you know his name, why can't you tell it to me? What are you afraid of?'

Miss Sharpe smiled delicately and prodded a flaming coal with her stick.

'On the contrary, Mr. Trevor. It seemed so obvious that I thought it was super-fluous to say more. However, if you cannot read the riddle, allow me to make it plain: the husband. Who else but the husband?'

'I am interested to know your reasons,' said Trevor coolly.

The old lady let out a brisk cackle at this riposte.

'Have it your own way! The men and women today have no stamina. They can't come to terms with life — or marriage, as the case may be — as it is. He is out of England for four years and when he comes home is surprised to find things changed. Expected life was like the fairy stories, and his castle and his princess had been fast asleep during the waiting years. While as for the child herself, she ran hither and thither like a frantic mouse, never knowing what she should do, and then doing it wrong.'

'Where can I find him?' asked Trevor gently, fitting the wire round the grate obediently.

She opened one eye like a parrot, and said with a parrot's raucous dreaminess:

'Where he is, I suppose.'

★ ★ ★

Another conversation that was not without significance was with the child, Priscilla, a brittle little fair girl with long straight hair and greenish-gray eyes.

He said: 'Hullo? Where are you off to?'

'Oh! Nowhere in particular,' she said nervously.

'Good! Not busy for ten minutes?'

'Well, yes, I am rather,' she said, sensing danger.

'Oh, a pity! I hoped you would show me round the grounds. I have to get the hang of things, and I expect you know I am a stranger to these parts.' He gave her his mild confiding smile.

She swung one foot.

'We-ell! ... ' She looked at him uncertainly.

'It would help me very much,' he said, and watched her look of uncertainty flash to eagerness, and knew that he had found the right chord to play, her desire to be of use, to be wanted. 'Tell me about yourself,' he said, as they walked away from the house. 'How long have you been here?'

'Nearly two years,' she said. 'Ever since Daddy died.'

'I'm sorry. In the war, was it?'

'He was shot down bombing the *Scharnhorst* and the *Gneisenau*. He had the D.S.O. and a posthumous V.C.' She looked at Trevor with a kind of fierce pride, and added: 'I had nowhere else to go, so Auntie Linda took me in.'

'Is your mother dead, too?'

'Mother left us, when I was six. I don't even know where she is now, so — ' the child shrugged her shoulders.

'It's a pity this should have happened just when you were getting used to your new home.'

'Yes, it is. It frightens me. I hope I'm not going to be a doomed sort of person, like saints, you know, who always have to have a lot of awful things happen to them, to tempt them and all that.'

'Still, in spite of being doomed you've been happy enough here, haven't you, with your aunt and your little cousins? I wonder if you can tell me what you did on the day she died. You understand that she was murdered, don't you? And that now we have to find who did it?'

'Of course I do. I'm not a child. And I can tell you exactly what happened that day, because I remember. It was the day I lost my bicycle. It was the day Nanny goes to see her married sister, and Aunt Linda asked me particularly after lunch if I'd mind looking after the children

46

because she had a headache and wanted to lie down for a bit. I was pushing Janey round in a barrow — oh, because she'd had a screaming fit over something or other. And then while I was looking for my bicycle you all came up and I thought it was because you knew it had been stolen. I wish you'd find it for me. The others won't believe it was stolen; they say it serves me right for being untidy and careless with my things; they say I'm always losing things. But I *didn't* lose it, because I know perfectly well where I left it.'

'You shall give the particulars to my sergeant and we'll look into it,' he promised.

'Thank you,' she said, intensely. 'Thank you.'

'Not at all, my dear child, not at all. I can see it means a lot to you; in a way, I imagine more than your aunt's death.'

'Oh!' she cried. She began to stammer, her eyes filled with tears and her face took on a badgered expression. 'You're against me, too, then! It isn't fair! I did care! I was awfully fond of her, I cried all that night, and I couldn't eat a thing yesterday. But the bicycle is my very own, it belongs to *me*.' She flushed. 'It was the last thing Daddy gave me . . . Anyway, she wasn't as good as you think. I know things — 'She looked flustered, and stopped provokingly. 'I won't tell you anymore,' she said, and ran off on her long spindly legs.

Inspector Trevor watched her with a puzzled frown; something about her reference to the child, Janey, having a crying fit troubled the back of his mind. He filed the query away in a corner of his brain and strolled back to the house to see if either of the men in the house had returned.

★   ★   ★

Though Trevor was not to know it, Mr. Marriot had radically altered in appearance since his daughter's death. The vigorous, vain old man had become really old, shaky, and gray in the face. Not only his clothes, but his very skin, seemed too large for him; his bones appeared to have shrunk within the flesh. He was almost exaggeratedly pathetic.

'I'm just a useless, old man,' was his constant burden.

'I've not yet had an opportunity, sir, of asking you for an account of your movements on that Wednesday afternoon,' Trevor was saying.

'My head,' said the old man apologetically, touching his forehead with palsied fingers. 'My memory isn't what it was. But I'll do my best to help you. We must do all in our power to catch this murderous rogue. Yes, yes. What were you saying, sir? You wanted to know what I had been doing with myself that afternoon. Nothing very particular, that I can recall. A little constitutional, don't you know, down to the village and back.'

'Can you remember the times, by any chance? Just as a guide, you know.'

'Mmm! Let me see now. I went out about three, I think, and returned just before five. I recollect that I waited in the paper shop, for the evening papers to arrive, and they come in on the four-thirty-eight like clockwork.'

49

'Did you come in the front entrance?'

'Naturally,' said Mr. Marriot, looking blank.

'I see. Can anyone confirm those times, do you know? Did anyone see you go or come?'

'I — I — Probably not,' said the old man, passing his hand over his scalp with a flurried movement.

'What did you do in the village all that time? See anyone you knew?'

'I may have spoken to one or two people . . . I — I'm afraid it's all gone now. Wiped away by my tragedy. It's been a terrible blow to me, you know. My little daughter! Really all I had to live for. My dear wife, you know, and my son, both gone before. I am left, a very lonely, very useless old man.'

'I deeply sympathize,' said Trevor. 'Never mind it now. Perhaps you will recall something later. You can't have spent two hours in the village just walking up and down its one street, after all.'

'No,' said the old man, looking down at his knees, turning over his hands resting on his knees. 'No, I suppose not.'

'Tell me a little about your daughter, will you? You will have understood her better than anyone else in the house, I am sure.'

'What sort of things do you want to know?' asked the old man, without looking up.

'Whether she was happy. Whether she had any worries. Any enemies. Why all these people were living in the house. Why her husband was not living here. Why — but those will do for a start.'

Mr. Marriot rubbed his palms together with nervous briskness.

'We helped, you see, we helped with the upkeep of the house, made our little contributions, that was why we were here. I speak now of my wife's sister, Miss Sharpe, and myself. Er — even that Austrian couple paid something into the kitty — very little, I imagine — Linda would never tell me how much. The little girl — that was a different thing of course; my boy's child.'

'Yes?' said the inspector encouragingly. Sergeant Drake in his corner turned over a fresh leaf in his notebook and waited.

51

After a pause Mr. Marriot said: 'Of course there were money troubles. Bound to be nowadays in a place this size. Can't afford the upkeep, you know; we're all in the same boat. Matter of fact, I've said all along it'll be a damn good thing when they sell the place, it's simply pouring good money down the drain — and all to no purpose, as I tell 'em. But of course Campion can't face the idea. He'll drag 'em all down, sooner than give it up. Wants the place for his sons, and all that sort of rot; when he can't even afford to send them to a decent school. Ah well, I'm only an old man, I can't keep up with things nowadays, but to my way of thinking it was asking too much of a young girl like Linda to expect her to keep a place like this going. It was killing her.' His eyes watered at the words, 'Brave little soul,' he muttered. 'The pity of it is that it was put on the market not long ago and she'd managed to sell it, and by a bit of cursed bad luck his lordship came home just before the deal went through, and not, I daresay, understanding the lay of the land, broke off negotiations at once. Bad show, that. Very bad show.' He began to fill a pipe.

'Is that what they quarreled about?'

'I daresay it would have been,' said Mr. Marriot disingenuously.

'Can you think of any reason why your daughter should have been murdered? Do you know of anyone who might have done it?'

'Now look here, I'm not accusing anybody,' he said uneasily. 'I know very little about my daughter's private affairs. I never interfered. I should prefer to say nothing.'

'What about these Hausers, Mr. Marriot? I understand that Mrs. Campion had asked them to leave — at rather short notice. And from what Mrs. Hauser said, I gather it was somewhat resented.'

'Heavens, you're not imagining that she was killed because she told the refugees she couldn't keep them any longer.'

'But Mrs. Hauser tells me that that is why her husband killed himself.'

'Does she, indeed?' commented Mr. Marriot, pressing his hands together earnestly and looking solemn. 'Does she . . . ? And are you suggesting that that little woman could have cruelly murdered my little girl by way of revenge, or — or to prevent herself from being thrown out?'

Trevor said nothing.

'It's preposterous! Surely you can see how silly and improbable it is, Inspector,' he said fretfully. 'Murders have been committed before now for very trifling causes. Murder is often silly and improbable — as well as vile.

'But in this instance . . . You see, Linda had asked us all to go. And I suppose her own family, on the face of it, had more reason to be aggrieved than an outsider. We none of us had anywhere to go, if it comes to that; it would not have been exactly convenient for us, either. However — ' He sighed and fell silent.

'Did she give any reason for wanting your sudden departure?'

'I gathered that she believed and hoped that if she had the place to herself, Campion would return.'

'Then there *had* been a quarrel? Had he left for good?'

'She thought not. She thought he meant to come back. She said he would never leave Hawkswood and the children, even if he didn't love her any more. Only, she said, there were too many people hanging about, interfering, causing friction. If she had him alone she could explain everything. She told me it wouldn't be for long. Just a few weeks, she said. She said she'd find a way of helping me if necessary. You understand it was not only a question of finding accommodation, though heaven knows that is hard enough these days by all accounts, but also the rising cost of living. I am already reduced to subsisting on my capital. It is not pleasant at my age. And the position was no better for Victoria — Miss Sharpe, that is. She has only a small annuity, I believe. And Priscilla, poor child, has nothing. So you see, we were none of us any better off than the Hausers.'

3

Priscilla's bicycle was discovered hidden in a clump of gorse bushes that dotted the common land on either side of the road for a mile or two beyond Hawkswood. This particular cluster of gorse bushes was about twenty yards back from the road and roughly a quarter of a mile distant from Hawkswood house following the road and the drive, but less cutting through the little wood at the edge of the estate.

The bicycle was muddy and scratched, but there were no fingerprints on it other than a few blurred ones of its owner's and other small ones that could only belong to one of the children.

Priscilla flushed with pleasure when Trevor restored it to her, even though its shining beauty was marred. She was perfectly positive that she had not taken the machine onto the Common and that, since Lionel had been more or less under her eye all that afternoon, and he was the only one of the children who could ride it, Lionel could not have left it there either. Yes, and she was equally positive that it was on the day of her aunt's death that the bicycle was lost — or stolen, as she preferred to call it.

'Who else could ride it?' Trevor asked.

'Do you think Auntie Tory might have ridden it down there and then tumbled into the bushes? I should like to have seen that! She makes everyone cry. Even Werner didn't get on with her very well, though he understood her, he said. He said — ' she groped back for the exact words and she uttered them with meticulous precision — 'her asperity was the old maiden's release from thwarted sexuality. He spoke very good English.'

'You liked him.'

'Oh, very much. He was awfully kind to me always. He said what I needed was a father-substitute, and then he used to laugh and say, what he needed was a child-substitute, and so we had better comfort each other. I did love him,' she sighed; 'more than Daddy, I sometimes think, because he always spoke seriously to me just as if I was a real person. You would think I was fated, wouldn't you, when everyone I love dies?'

'Unhappily, there are very many of us today who have lost all those we love. But you are still young enough to find other people to love — even though you don't expect it — just as you found Werner Hauser,' Trevor said mildly.

She said with a curious nonchalance:

'Oh, I'm reconciled to losing Werner because he wanted to go. He wasn't happy, you know. He couldn't have been, could he? He said I was the only one he could talk to, the only one who understood . . . '

'Mrs. Hauser didn't?'

'Oh, he did love her, because she is so beautiful, you know. But she didn't *understand*. She could only live in the beautiful past, he said; she felt that he had failed her because they had been forced to leave their own land and live in poverty like nobodies among strangers. All his adoration was not enough, he said; he no longer satisfied her. It used to make me cry to hear him.'

'Poor child,' said Trevor gently, 'it wasn't fair, was it? Taking advantage of you emotionally.'

She did not quite understand what his words meant, but the unexpected tone of sympathy brought the ready tears welling up. Her greenish eyes, enlarged and stiff-lashed with tears, gave her a queer kind of dignity that held a promise of future beauty.

She burst out suddenly: 'Auntie Linda gave me the bicycle, and Daddy was killed in London in an ordinary air raid like anybody else. He wasn't even a soldier . . . I *do* tell lies. Werner says — said, I mean — that it's a hunger for approval and it's quite natural in the circumstances; having to build my own background now, I invent what doesn't exist. But all this that I've been telling you isn't lies, it's the truth. I just wanted you to know.'

'It was nice of you to tell me. I hope that means we're going to be friends.' Poor moppet, he thought, is *this* fair? And sighed. After a decent pause, Trevor briskly changed the subject by asking her to tell him what it was she had hinted the other day that she knew about her Aunt Linda to her detriment. Priscilla looked embarrassed.

'I don't know how to say it,' she said, sniffing and blowing her nose. 'It was wrong of me ever to have mentioned it. Uncle Edmund would say it was disloyal; I see that now. But I didn't know who else to go to, as darling Werner was already dead, and really and truly I couldn't have shown it to Uncle Edmund, even if he had been here. It would have hurt him so much.' She kept her gaze fixed on her fingers she was carefully plaiting.

Trevor said: 'What would?'

'Why, the letter of course. I thought and thought. I didn't like to ask Grandpa's advice. And I wouldn't have shown it to Aunt Tory for the world. I didn't know what I ought to do with it. And so in the end I asked Ilse. Was it wrong?'

'How can I tell? I don't know what was in the letter. What was it about?'

'I don't know,' she said hastily. 'I didn't

read it. Only the beginning. Then I saw it was private, so I didn't read any more. I just folded it up and put it in my pocket.'

'Why not simply have left it where it was, if you didn't know to whom it belonged?'

'Don't you see,' she said impatiently, 'it wasn't the sort of letter to be left lying about. And of course I knew who it belonged to, isn't that just what I'm saying? It belonged to Aunt Linda. At least, it was meant for her. But Ivor had written it, so perhaps it really belonged to him. Only I couldn't possibly have given it back to him; I just couldn't you know. And I couldn't give it to Aunt Linda, either. Don't you understand, she would have been so ashamed! It's horrible to find a grown-up doing something they shouldn't, it makes you feel prickly all over.'

'And what did Mrs. Hauser say?'

'She said she'd take care of it; it would be safe in her hands, she said, and I wasn't to bother my head any more about it. 'Forget it,' she said, 'forget it, my child.' So I tried not to think any more about it;

and anyway, there really wasn't anything else I could do,' she concluded primly.

'If I understand you right, you think that Ivor Campion and your Aunt Linda were lovers. Is that it?'

She pinkened.

'Yes,' she whispered.

'Any other evidence, beside the letter, of which you only saw the beginning?'

'I don't know what you mean,' she said warily.

'Dear me, how am I to put it? You understand what it is, to be lovers? Do you understand?'

'Of course I do,' she said indignantly with a furious toss of her head that sent her blonde hair flying ... flying to conceal her flushed cheek. 'Besides, Ivor is Uncle's best friend, and that's why he's here. And it always is the best friend, isn't it, who betrays the husband's trust?'

'In books, you mean?'

'Aren't books true?' she said innocently.

'Oh, Priscilla, Priscilla! What a dangerous girl you are!' sighed Trevor.

'Hullo, sir, what have you there?' said Sergeant Drake when Trevor strolled into the station that evening.

'This,' he said, holding the prize up but away from Drake's grasp, 'this is the object for which some person or persons unknown were searching in Mrs. Campion's room. Interesting, eh? It was found in the false bottom of the rosewood box.'

'But we looked there, sir, didn't we, and there was only a lot of rubbishy recipes and receipts and such.'

'I didn't mean to imply that I had found it in the rosewood box, my dear fellow. It was Mrs. Hauser who won the lucky dip.'

'What is it?'

'Letters. She had them in her sponge-bag, of course.'

'Hers, are they then?'

'Oh, no, Drake, no. Quite the contrary, as Mrs. Potter would say. They were addressed to the late-lamented by Ivor Campion apparently. I cannot but think that Mrs. Hauser must have rather a nasty nature. Vicious, would you say? Or

63

simply, an eye to the main chance?'

'How did *she* know they were in the rosewood box?'

'Is that what they call womanly intuition, Drake? Or perhaps it was simply trial and error. I knew she'd been at it of course, because of the bronze hairpin. Remember? She'd bent it to pick the lock of the false drawer. Too clever for her own good, that madam.'

'Rum idea, though, to write letters when you're living in the same house,' Drake mused.

Trevor, turning over the envelopes, said: 'He wasn't at Hawkswood all the time. Look, here's one from S.W. 1, here's another from Surrey, two more from London. The ones written in the house have only got her name typewritten on the front. Reasonably cautious, you see. He would write, my unromantic Drake, because he found it difficult to be alone with her, with few opportunities to say all the things he wanted to get said — which, after all, are only the things all lovers say. Or were they? . . . We shall see!'

He pulled out a stiff white sheet

inscribed with a vigorous black lettering. Hardly the precise exquisite hand he had imagined to be Ivor's, and he turned to the end to see the signature — merely a devil-may-careish 'I.'

Two A.M. (he read):

Insomnia is my pleasure now as well as my torment, for all these empty hours can be filled with you. Only, if I slept I might dream of you, and my dreams might be more satisfying than the reality. It isn't that I want to touch you, Linda, my beautiful Linda. If you came to me now, at this hour of the night, I would only adore . . . Ah, but I tremble at the thought! You've no idea how I feel about you, my lovely girl; you're all that I never believed in . . .

'And so on and so on,' groaned Trevor, with paragraphs arresting his eye . . .

. . . I would cheerfully forfeit my right hand (as well as my right foot!) to make you happy, but all the same, and without any thought of self, I say, FORGET

HIM! FORGET HIM! Believe me, darling, he's not worth one of your tears . . .

. . . Why do you avoid my eyes so persistently? How have I offended you? You are angry with me. Is it because I kissed you in the garden? But, my dear, it was simply out of gratitude to you for all your sympathy and goodness. How could you think otherwise? Don't you know how deeply I respect you? Believe me, you are not by any means in the same category as the girls I kiss. You are Edmund's wife. I know that, with my reputation, that hardly seems adequate to protect your honor; but strangely enough that has all changed. My feeling for you is one of sincerest friendship, truest devotion, and a very humble hope that you will represent to me the pure love of the sister I should have had . . .

'It's easy enough to date them, isn't it, even though he hasn't. This is obviously one of the first, or the first. Sweet-spoken young blackguard, ain't he?' said Trevor with relish. He turned the pile over. 'Here's one!'

You are cross with me; I can see it in your averted cheek, and your little roughened fingers tapping on the arm of your chair. And I don't care! It made me want to laugh. Oh, Linda, you little fool, you little darling fool! You are jealous! All because I flirted with Ilse. Do you really think I care tuppence for, or even like, that tarty little Austrian egotist? Don't you know by now that the image which gives me no peace at night or day is of a thin girl with long black hair . . . ?

'It's as good as a diary, isn't it? Tells you everything you want to know.'

'Of course, if the husband knew . . . ' Drake said tentatively.

'Oh, quite! He's the obvious person, isn't he? So everyone is at pains to point out to me. It's quite a commonplace nowadays for men to come out of the Services, find their wives have been or are being unfaithful, and kill them.'

Drake drew a pencil line down the center of the page.

'And he'll say a red mist seemed to

float in front of him and he didn't know what he was doing, and when he saw what he'd done he was frightened, or he lost his memory and he's been wandering about the countryside . . . This country is getting just like France to my mind, sir; no morals; and all this *crime passionnel* stuff.'

Looking at his sergeant, Trevor thought, the English character never changes; but he did not knock him. He said: 'It's habit. People get in the habit of killing during a war, and afterwards, the customary inhibitions no longer act with the same force and certainty. All the same, it won't go down very well with a jury if he tries the 'red mist' plea. We know she was killed about half-past three or four and she certainly wasn't dropped over the stairs until after five. Not much 'red mist' there, eh?'

'I rather think you've got something there, sir, if you don't mind my saying so. It does look bad, doesn't it?'

Trevor laughed.

'Always bearing in mind, my good Drake that this is all supposition only

. . . Nevertheless,' he added a moment later, 'he does not make it look very well for himself, staying away like this.'

PART TWO

4

He was a man of about thirty-six years, with a tough, sturdy frame, muscular and lean; there was nothing rangy about his limbs; they were close-knit and disciplined in their movements, so that even without his uniform you might guess him to be a soldier. His face was square, frowning and pugnacious as a schoolboy's; his hair was watered down to the color of old wood but the freckles on his skin and the light hazel brown of his deep-set eyes betrayed its natural reddish tinge. His expression was wooden, unvarying, even now when he was alone, though certain lights could lend his stubborn, shut-in face a look of weary melancholy, could make him look unexpectedly, touchingly frail in his ill-fitting khaki, as small boys at their prep schools look unnervingly fragile. It was as deceptive an appearance in the one case as the other; he was inexorably tough . . . even now, staring about him at the desolation, like the desolation in his heart.

It was for him exactly like a nightmare, walking up the long drive home. It was the more curious, because the return to Hawkswood had been a recurring nightmare of Edmund's wherever he had been during the last four years, in prison camp, in the jungle of Central Borneo, even in the Technicolor brilliance of the States; only in these dreams Hawkswood was always just the same as when he left it and the nightmare part of it was in the awakening.

The recollection of those dreams tinged the present scene with their unreality, as though this too were just one more jest of the mind. The rank, filled ditches by the wayside, the overgrown hedges too thin at the base, the wilderness of grass where used to undulate fine-mown turf, the drive shaggy with weeds, indicated years of neglect. The elegant Palladian face of the building itself looked hopelessly dilapidated and uncared for; creeper obscuring two of the upper rooms gave it a rakish cast, a drunken raffish look that was faintly obscene.

He walked on, slowly, round the side of the house . . .

A little girl with a towel about her shoulders was running excitedly round and round a small boy crouched over something on the grass. Beyond, he saw two short stout legs and an all-enveloping towel, and Linda. Linda, sitting on her heels with her back turned toward him. Linda, in the same blue cotton frock she was wearing the last time he saw her, four years ago, on his embarkation leave. Linda, the one unchanged creature in a changed world. Her black hair hung untidily about her shoulders in a weary shoulder-length bob, like a schoolgirl's. She was crooning to the little boy (it must be Charles under that towel, the one he had never seen, who had been born while he was abroad after that last embarkation leave); she crooned to him, as she rubbed his hair dry, in a pretty off-the-key voice that grated on the ear the way ultra-sweetness sets the teeth on edge.

The little running girl was the first to notice the intruder. She stood very still a moment, surveying him, and then said in an inquisitive cajoling voice:

'Hallo?'

'Hallo!' said Edmund.

At the sound of his voice the girl in the blue frock swiftly turned and stared at him with something like dismay in her face.

He said: 'Hallo, Linda!'

She went white. Then scarlet.

She said incredulously:

'*Edmund!*'

Then she flung herself against him, thin body and coltish limbs as light as a bird in his arms, black hair flying. Linda, her voice muffled against his collar, said: 'I wasn't expecting you so soon, Eddie. You ought to have let me know. Nothing's ready, and I did so want to have every-thing looking extra-specially nice for you. I meant to get my hair done, and I wanted to dress up, and do my nails and all that . . . I can't help crying, to think you've come home at last and will never go away again!' she snuffled.

'What a charming way to put it! I'd forgotten your famous tact, dear!'

She began to laugh, and blew her nose. She said, rather shakily, to the children: 'Do you know who this is?'

'Yes. It's our father. Hallo,' said Jane with an impudent face. Jane hesitated and then turned upside down defiantly and stood on her hands. 'Look at *me*,' she piped shrilly. 'Look at *me!*'

'I can do that,' said Oliver quickly, and running forward a few steps he pressed the top of his head on the grass, flung up his legs halfheartedly, and fell over on his side.

'Very good, darling,' said Linda.

'But it wasn't,' Edmund objected.

Linda said hastily at his ear: 'I know. But Jane is better than he is at everything physical and she's a year younger; it's so bad for his morale. I like to encourage him a little.'

Edmund said firmly, crushing down an all-too-familiar feeling of irritation: 'It can't be very good for his morale to tell him he has done a thing well when he hasn't done it at all. It only makes a fool of him if he believes it. But as he looks quite an intelligent little boy I don't suppose he does believe it. In that case, he knows you've lied to him. That's not good for his morale either.'

'You're quite right,' she said, with all her old devastating facility for evading an issue. 'But let's not bother about them now; I want to have you to myself for just a minute. I want to have a good look at your ugly old face, because I can't believe it's really you at last. I want to see if you've changed. I want you to tell me if you're glad to be home. Do you know you haven't kissed me yet?' She held up her face, innocently.

'I know,' he said, and bent his head; for it was easier to touch her unfamiliar mouth with his lips than to answer her terrible questions or look into her eyes.

Her thin shoulders felt brittle under his hands, and he dropped them to his sides with an odd feeling of guilt.

'Oughtn't I to meet my youngest son?' he suggested.

Charles, addressing his invisible audience with Churchillian rhetoric, ignored Linda's coaxing: 'This is Daddy, darling.'

'My Daddy's coming to-mollow!' He waved them away like tiresome wasps. 'My Daddy's coming to-mollow!' he repeated, trundling away like a stout old

Georgian gentleman.

They laughed a little, insincerely, as though they were playing a scene in a film.

'I'm not surprised really,' he said, with his eyes on the ground. 'I don't feel like a father to them myself. They're just little strange children that don't seem any part of me. Where's Lionel? I can remember him, at any rate; though of course he won't remember me either.'

'He's gone to the village with Priscilla — ' She broke off and looked frightened, as if she had said something she had meant not to say.

He said of course:

'Who's Priscilla?'

She said hurriedly, inartistically:

'Oh, darling! George's girl. She is such a help. Especially just now while Nanny's laid up with her bad leg. She's in hospital, poor darling, did you know? I can't remember if I told you. You'll have to go and see her, Eddie, she'll be thrilled to bits.'

'Who's George?'

She looked reproachful.

'Darling, my brother! You can't have forgotten. I told you he'd been killed. It was dreadfully unf-fortunate,' she stammered, her face whitening. 'And so I said poor little Priscilla could stay here. She had nowhere else to go, poor child.'

'Of course,' he said in mild surprise. 'You did quite right. I'm very glad you have her. I daresay she was company for you.'

'Company?' said Linda in a vague nervous voice, not looking at him. 'Oh, yes.' She twisted her hands together. 'I did write and tell you Daddy was here, darling. I never knew whether you got half my letters. I knew you wouldn't *mind*. Where else could he go, once George was dead? And then of course I didn't like him being in London during all those raids. It wasn't right. It worried me dreadfully. It was much *easier* for me to have him here safely under my eye, you do see that, don't you . . . ? And Great-Aunt Tory, who you don't know, Eddie; she was an aunt of Mother's. She's a perfect pet really, and completely independent, although she's about eighty.'

80

'Well, well,' he said brightly. 'Who else? Don't tell me that's the lot.'

'Eddie darling, you're not to be beastly,' she said, girlishly tracing the crown on his shoulder with a slim forefinger. 'There's only Nanny Potter, who you asked to come yourself, and the Hausers. They're an Austrian refugee couple.'

'I didn't realize from your letters that all these people were actually living in the house, I'm afraid.'

She said evasively:

'Oh, well, perhaps you never got the letters. And anyhow, nothing matters now you're back. They can all go away if you don't like them.' Again her face changed color, as she added: 'It will only be for a time, anyway.'

It was not worthwhile pursuing the subject any further. He had suddenly a longing to get out of his hatefully familiar khaki, to boil himself peaceably in the vast old-fashioned bath upstairs for three-quarters of an hour, and then to put on his 'demob' suit which a grateful Army had bestowed on him as a parting gift.

'This is home,' he thought, wandering

down the familiar corridors with their high cracked ceilings. ('That was done when the buzz bomb fell,' Linda explained, seeing his glance. 'There's a huge crater in the park.')

'This is home,' he repeated, standing in the big unused drawing room with the chandelier hidden in its holland bag and sheets over the furniture, staring at the ghostly patches here and there marking the walls. ('We had to sell the Van Dyke, Eddie. I couldn't bear to tell you in a letter. And the little Turner you loved so. I didn't want to, I wanted to keep it, knowing what it meant to you, but I had a good offer, really good, and they all said I'd be mad not to take it. Eddie, if I've done wrong, you'll just have to forgive me. You know I don't understand anything about these things, and I have to take the advice of people who do. What was to be done? The Bank were pressing. I had to find two thousand. They said I was very lucky to get seventeen hundred for the Turner and four-fifty for the Van Dyke.' Her eyes were anxious, very blue.)

'This is home,' he reminded himself

later in the morning room, feeling like an alien among his guests. They were wonderfully patronizing to him, all of them. All of them, except Priscilla, that is, who leaned shyly up against the bookcase in silence.

'Glad to have you back with us again, my boy,' said his father-in-law encouragingly, looking as handsome as paint with his fine old face and keen blue eyes, his splendid carriage and unshakable conceit. 'This calls for a little celebration, what? A bottle of pop! Our little frugal Linda refused to let us crack a bottle on V-E Day. Isn't she canny? She must have been keeping it for your homecoming, the little monkey!'

Werner Hauser, the Austrian refugee, with a worn tortured face and streaks of white among his black hair, was being sensitively polite to him. Edmund tried hard to pay attention to what he was saying. The other side of the room, sitting exquisitely still, was his wife, 'who had been a countess and now couldn't adjust herself,' he remembered. Her mouth was like a purple snapdragon in her pale face. Her eyes were large and haunting, mahogany-colored like her hair. She arrested the eye. She sat there quietly, not speaking, her sensual regard fixed on him calmly, so that he was conscious of it all the time. Werner ran his long thin fingers through his hair and went on explaining carefully, in his ill-accented recondite English, the franchise system of Austria.

The old lady said acidly:

'I should think he'd heard enough about Germany to last him a lifetime.'

Werner Hauser said very politely:

'Excuse me, Miss Sharpe, that I should contradict you. We were speaking of my country — Austria.'

'Same thing.'

'Excuse me. It is not at all the same thing; no more than England and America are the same thing because they speak the same language. Austria was an occupied territory as much as was Denmark or where you will.'

'Well, we don't want to hear about it, anyway,' she said, decisively, with her sweet old lady's smile.

'This is home,' thought Edmund, gazing round at their unfamiliar faces as he raised his shallow glass with the others in a toast.

Hesitantly, Linda said:

'Look, Eddie, you won't mind, will you? The Hausers are in our room. It seemed the most sensible thing at the time, because I converted the old schoolroom for myself when the children had measles; and after, I found it so convenient to be near them, and so much more restful for Nanny that I stayed on up there: We'll move it round of course tomorrow. But just for tonight if you wouldn't mind sharing a rather small bed . . . ' she said, blushing violently.

'Oh, I don't want to disturb you, my dear. I'll doss down anywhere.' He could have smiled with relief. 'I'm so tired I could sleep the clock round anyway,' he added kindly, seeing her trembling lips.

And indeed it was an enormous luxury to be alone and quiet in a room by himself. No more need for pretense. No need to mask his feelings of distress and irritation. There was time to think of what it all meant. Time to think about the future. If there was to be a future. He sat yawning on the end of the bed, pulling odds and ends out of his pockets and tossing them onto the rather ugly, black, veneered-walnut chest of drawers. In the same desultory manner he discarded from his mind the unrelated fragments of his day.

Edmund (lying sleepless on the bed despite his protestations of fatigue) groaned, thinking of Genevieve. He had met her just over a year ago, when he was in the States in connection with some of the training of American troops for D-Day.

It was at one of these banquets for the fostering of international goodwill that he was introduced to Genevieve. He did notice that she was very beautiful, with the intolerable glitter of someone devoted to her own perfecting. He thought her utterly detestable — the kind of woman for whom he had nothing but contempt, a contempt that placed her in value beneath, say, a good professional lousy whore with her front teeth knocked out.

He was very remotely polite; you might just say that he was polite to her. But not attentive. He was so far removed from the urbanites of civilization that he could think of nothing to say to her. His silence was as much a defensive measure as anything else. If he did not speak she would eventually go away. Her voice was soft, very low; pleasant to hear. He listened to her voice rather than to what she was saying.

She was dutifully valiant in her attempts to interest this dreary Englishman in his shabby uniform, looking as though he had left his body here but had taken his spirit five thousand miles away. She shot him a quick glance, but he was not looking at her and she was so unaccustomed to not being looked at that that astonished her. She thought him decidedly unattractive, gaunt and rather ill-looking in the artificial light, in his unbecoming khaki, with his khaki-colored hair and spattering of khaki-colored freckles, and very likely khaki-colored eyes if one could see them. Or a very weak, watery blue, perhaps. That would be even worse. She noticed that if she did not speak neither did he. She made desperate signals with her eyes across the room. They could not stand there like two dumb ninnies. Having exhausted all her small talk, she was obliged to start asking him questions — about himself. Men always loved to talk about themselves; every woman knew that.

Did he like New York?

Did he like Washington?

Did he like California?

Where did he live in England?

Kent? Oh, she adored Kent. (That ought to fetch out the snapshots of home and his fat bouncing wife — a jolly good sort!)

Was he married?

He said, No, abruptly. And then flushed, and blurted hastily:

'Look here, you're not drinking anything. You must let me get you a drink.' And he plunged away into the thick of the crowd and out of sight.

With her beautiful manners it never entered her head that he did not mean to return, and she waited there patiently until the person who had introduced them touched her on the elbow and adjured her to 'Snap out of it!' and inquired what she had done with the major.

'He's gone to get me a drink!'

'I doubt it.'

'How do you mean, you doubt it?'

'Have you any idea how long you've been standing here waiting? My guess is that he has passed by this way but once.'

Genevieve was incredulous. Such a thing hadn't happened to her since the age of fourteen when she wore a disfiguring brace on her teeth. She did waste a moment or two's thought on him, wondering why he had run away; then she forgot him entirely.

It seemed inevitable that they should from time to time find themselves at the same functions. The first time she was embarrassed to death to find herself sitting next to him at a concert of chamber music. Embarrassed for his sake, of course. Needlessly, as it happened. He didn't turn a hair, just made her a cool polite little bow, as she made her escape at the end of the first movement and just turned back at the door for a quick glance. So that later she was compelled to wonder whether he really had recognized her, or had simply bowed because he had caught her staring.

It arrived at the point where it set her nerves on edge only to see him when she walked into a room. It could spoil an evening for her, merely being aware of his captious critical regard watching her. Sometimes she forced herself to address him, in the attempt to break down this antagonism she sensed in him — or was it in herself? Impossible to tell, for, however well-intentioned she thought she was, her pleasantries always ended in a brisk, ungraceful exchange of discourtesies.

And then, by one of the maddening arrangements of Fate (her own car in dock, and a day of pouring rain), she found herself sharing a taxi with him. In dogged silence. There was doubtless thunder in the air. At any rate, the atmosphere in the taxi was electrical, frighteningly tense. The interior of the cab seemed very dark, very close; for a moment Genevieve feared she was going to faint — which would be an unbearable humiliation. She tried to relax, to breathe deeply . . . The taxi lurched, and she fell against him. 'I beg your pardon,' she said in a stifled voice. To regain her balance she caught at his hand, and at once a fiery anguish ran all over her body, piercing her breasts, turning her bowels to water — a sensation she had never known before. Her mouth was dry. His hand tightened on hers. She was pressed against him, could feel his coarse hairy serge against her cheek and feel his heart hammering against his side. For some reason this made tears prick her eyes. Only when his mouth closed on hers did she stop trembling and was lost in a whirl of liquid gold and sank down into a velvety darkness . . .

The taxi rattled into the curb and jerked to a stop.

The major said breathlessly:

'I don't even know your name . . . '

She said primly:

'Mrs. Hamilton. Genevieve Hamilton.' And laughed weakly.

'Oh, you're married!' he exclaimed in dismay.

'No, I'm a widow.' In a sudden panic she began fumbling her things together. 'I must go.'

'When am I going to see you again?'

'I don't think I want to see you again,' she said as inoffensively as possible. But he brushed that aside.

'That's nonsense of course. Have dinner with me tonight?'

'Oh, that would be quite impossible, I'm afraid,' she said in her gentle positive way. His hand closed on her wrist, and again that magical touch arrested her.

'Tonight?' he repeated.

She thought, *I must be out of my mind! Why, I don't even like him!*

She said in a hurried muffled voice, as she bent her head to descend from the taxi:

'Call for me at eight.'

★ ★ ★

They were desperately enamored. A glance was enough to set them aflame. It was a queer-enough affair, when one came to think of it; they were so very different from one another that they would always be virtually strangers. Beyond the bare facts of their lives, they had little enough to exchange. They were neither of them talkative people (though Genevieve had her own polished veneer of social chatter), so there was, so to speak, no conversation. Not that either of them felt the lack of it. They were absorbedly satisfied with each other's mere physical presence, and could share a contented or murmuring silence for hours.

She spoke sometimes of her childhood. She came of an old and exceedingly wealthy Philadelphian family of Quakers, with all the Quakers' passion for industry and propriety. She was just a little girl to whom nothing had ever happened — nothing, that is, was not utterly becoming and respectable. She had been amazingly sheltered from the harsh glare of reality.

She almost never mentioned her husband, who also had been fabulously wealthy, and as practically innocent as herself. He had been young and ineffectual and sweet. She was nineteen when she married him and he was twenty-two. They were married for six years. And then one summer he was drowned sailing off Cape Cod. They had no children. She was now thirty-one.

As for Edmund, he spoke seldom of the past and never of the future. Some ulterior discretion, or maybe it was some capricious inhibition, prevented his mentioning Linda's name. With the Englishman's rectitude it is on the whole unlikely that he was deliberately trying to deceive her; it is more reasonable to suppose that the same power that forbids painful memory sealed his tongue.

And then one day, he had been downtown to collect his mail and was in her apartment reading it while he waited for her, when out of a fold of blue-gray paper spluttered half a dozen snapshots. She entered and saw them lying about his feet as he skimmed frowning through the letter. He stuffed it away hastily when he saw her and rose.

She said, as he kissed her:

'Watch out, darling! Don't tread on them!'

And together they bent to collect them.

She saw pictures of small children in an English garden, tumbling about with dogs and cats, laughing, except one boy, the biggest, who wore a scowl; that somehow turned her heart over in her breast. In one photo he was frowning into the sun with a kitten in his arms, and his freckles were plain to see.

'That's Lionel,' he said over her shoulder. 'The other two trying to pull 'Sausage' in half are Oliver and Jane. The little fair boy is called Charles, I understand.' He added queerly: 'I've never seen him.'

Staring at Lionel blindly, she could think of nothing to say but:

'He is the image of you, isn't he?'

'He is supposed to favor me, I believe.'

She turned away, groping clumsily in her case for a cigarette, fumbling with a lighter. When she was sure of her voice, she said, without looking at him, in a dead-steady expressionless voice:

'Is he your child?'

The question astonished him. He had frankly forgotten that all that chapter of his life was hidden from her. He said:

'Of course he is, Gene.' And added, as if it was an explanation: 'They are all my children.'

She made a small involuntary exclamation, a sound that might have been caused by the swift sharp sting of a flame.

'What is the matter?' he asked, and put out his hand.

But she retreated from him and said shakily:

'You lied to me!'

'What?'

'You lied to me! You told me you weren't married!'

'I did? When?'

She stammered:

'Oh, don't . . . Don't . . . How can you . . . ? The very first time we met . . . I remember it perfectly. Now I see! That was why you disappeared. You had lied and you were ashamed — '

He looked confused.

'Yes, I remember it now,' he murmured. 'You asked me if I was married and I said 'No'. I can't think why. I felt such a fool. I think I just wanted to get away from you. I have always loathed being questioned.'

'But you could have told me later. God, you had a hundred opportunities! Why did you never mention that you had a wife when I was telling you about Paul?'

A sudden thought struck her and drove some color back into her cheeks. 'Or is she dead, too?'

He pulled out the blue-gray letter and stared at it.

'No, she's not dead . . . Gene, I shall never be able to explain to you what prompted me to keep the truth from you, because I don't know myself. I think perhaps it was a desire to prolong the fantasy of my life with you by keeping out as much of the real world outside us as possible. The desire to be happy combined with the fear that a chance word might lose it.'

She essayed an ironical laugh. She shut her eyes and put her hands to her face: 'How sordid it is! How unspeakable? I feel so degraded!' She shuddered, and added quickly: 'Go now, please.'

He went at once, without another word.

She had not quite expected that. Not that she was not sincere in her command, but she thought at least he would protest, explain, extenuate, do something to make her feel better toward her own outraged morality. He had left her to wrestle with her discomfiture alone. And her misery was increased by her shameful, heart-aching longing for him.

For two days she was in an agony that she thought would send her out of her mind. She hoped it would. And then, on the evening of the second day, Edmund turned the key in the lock and entered. He stood there looking at her. He said nothing. He was deadly pale. The French clock loudly ticked the silence away. Then, with nothing said, they were frantically in each other's arms . . .

By mutual consent they kept off the subject for several days, but it lay like a sword between them. They were sad, distrustful, guarded with one another.

Once he broke the quietness to say, a little breathlessly, as though he had been running:

'If I ever get my divorce, will you marry me?'

She said almost irritably:

'I don't know, I can't answer you now.'

There were moments when she decided that she really hated him. He seemed so utterly unimaginative and insensitive. He had evidently no idea how great the shock had been to discover that he had lied to her so successfully, so shamelessly. To have four children and never to mention the fact to the person you were most intimate with revealed a callousness in his character that was terrifying: a callousness toward her *and* toward his children. Or an obstinate grim secrecy that might even be worse.

And then to try and smooth things over by asking her calmly to marry him in the event that he was divorced! Prepared apparently at the crack of Genevieve's whip to abandon his wife and their four small children, the eldest of whom was barely seven years old ... Genevieve could not restrain a shiver.

He put out a hand in the dark and touched her:

'What is it, sweetheart?' he said. 'Cold?'

She dropped the back of her wrist across her mouth and said in a stilled voice:

'Cold, to my very marrow.'

'You're trembling!'

She moved out of his embrace. She would not make a scene because she was not the sort of person who could. Scenes were never any part of her life. She did not know how to be other than lovely and graceful and dignified. She had perhaps never in her whole life had occasion to lose her temper. Any display of unbridled emotion was abhorrent to her. In her sheltered life, angry shouted words, even though not addressed to her, were like blows on her body; a blow would be as unthinkable as death itself. So one was civilized, restrained, mannerly, even in despair. It was a similar restraint in Edmund that had showed up so well against her braggart compatriots. Just as she never let Edmund or anyone else see her with a hair out of place, her whole person as exquisitely contrived as a Fabergé enamel, so in her life she could not endure anything the least disapprobatory. The world, which was Genevieve's conscience, would not excuse her or believe that she had not known she was engaged in an enterprise that was amazingly squalid and scandalous for a person in her position. (Her mind's eye shrank from the imagined headlines and publicity.) Edmund had placed her in an invidious position and it was that she could not forgive.

Edmund did not revert to the question of marriage. It was she who brought it up incidentally by asking him incredulously if he had no feeling for his children at all.

He was amazed at her.

'How could I have? I'm hardly aware that they exist. I haven't been home for three years, you know, and in the last five years I've had two home-leaves — one of a week and one of ten days. The only one I've really seen is Lionel, and he was only a baby when I went to the war. They're their mother's business, not mine. It's no one's fault, but what else can you expect? What can 'Daddy' mean to them, after all? It is absurd to be sentimental about these hard irresistible facts.'

'You speak like a monster! Doesn't it occur to you that they need you?' she protested.

'I don't think I'm particularly unnatural really. They've had to do without me

101

all these years, and it may be another year or two yet. I can't see why I'm obliged to give you up for their sake, or how it can benefit them. Provided I see that their voracious maws are well filled and their growing bodies clothed, haven't I done all that can be expected of me as a father? I'm not particularly fond of children, you know. It was Linda who wanted a large family. After Oliver I said, no more. Linda was still so young, it was absurd. When the war came I wanted children less than ever. It had the opposite effect on Linda. She wanted more children and more, to help her forget my absence, she said — '
He cut himself short.

'Is she pretty?'

'I think so,' he answered after a moment's thought.

Well, what else did you expect him to say? Genevieve asked herself.

She found herself asking the same questions Cleopatra had asked about Anthony's wife, Octavia. Twisting the knife in the wound, she asked:

'What is she like?'

'Oh . . . Black hair. Blue eyes. I'm no

good at describing people . . . She's a simple sort of person. Very young.'

'Younger than me?' asked Genevieve, turning her face a little further from the light.

He looked across at her in vague speculation.

'I've no idea how old you are. Linda will be twenty-eight next January. But I didn't mean in years; I meant she's young in her ways. Unsophisticated.'

'Yes, I see,' she said, folding her hands in her lap, bowing her head. It was hopeless, hopeless . . .

But when he was obliged to return to Europe, the anguish of separation and the fear of his being killed in one of the theaters of war effectively banished all rancor between them. More than half believing they would never meet again, Genevieve promised, promised faithfully, to marry him directly the war was over, or as soon as he was free. It seemed the smallest sop to Fate she could provide.

'And write to me, darling,' she cried. 'Swear you'll write!'

All women weep, all women say the

same things when their lovers sail off to fight. Yet somehow life goes on. And mostly they forget. But sometimes they do not.

5

It is hard to decide now whether Linda made a serious blunder in not telling Edmund the facts at once or whether she was cleverly guileful to let it unfold itself piece by piece before his appalled eyes, as the turn of events called them up. For the fact is, his affairs were in an atrocious state — worse even than he had imagined in his bloodiest hours. Even before the war he had been dropping a steady six hundred a year on the estate, and by 1941 it had risen sharply to twelve hundred and thence, under Linda's adroit mismanagement, had easily turned the two-thousand mark and more. That was why Linda had been obliged to sell some of the pictures; also his mother's old-fashioned tiara of diamonds (a hideous affair that Linda knew she would never wear; she didn't care for jewelry, anyway).

Edmund turned over the rent books, studied the accounts, frowned over the bills.

'I kept everything for you to see,' Linda said complacently.

'But I *don't* see ... ' muttered Edmund. 'Here's over three thousand pounds' worth of things you sold, and where did the money go?'

'To the Bank of course. I told you.'

'But according to this balance sheet the overdraft isn't reduced by a penny. I don't understand.'

'Isn't it?' she said stupidly, with an anxious face.

'Where has the money gone?' he repeated on a higher note.

She could think of nothing to say, and she burst into tears.

Edmund's heart sank.

'Well, it was George, poor darling,' she began 'He came to me in a frightful jam; they were going to call a creditor's meeting or something — you know how stupid I am about business, Eddie! Anyway, he needed three thousand pounds desperately, he said. And who else was there for him to turn to? It would be only for a few weeks, he said, and he explained why. Of course I said I couldn't possibly. And he assured me that there was no risk whatsoever. I can't remember all he said now, but I know at the time it was all quite clear. Still, Eddie, I did tell him I hadn't got that amount of money — nor anything like it. I told him I wouldn't know where to lay my hands on three thousand — in cash. And then, you see, Eddie, he said he didn't want me to give him any money, he only wanted me to guarantee him for that amount at his Bank. I didn't see how I could refuse, Eddie; my own brother. He swore it was perfectly safe . . . And I suppose it would have been. Only, three days later, he was killed by a cheat-raider, coming out of an air-raid shelter just after the All Clear . . . So, you see, Eddie, I had to meet the guarantee,' she ended disarmingly.

'But honestly, what else could I have done?' she kept saying unhappily. 'You'd have done the same yourself if you'd been here. I know you would. You're my generous Eddie.'

He said nothing. It was not worth answering.

And still, it appeared, the Bank were

urgently pressing him to reduce his over-draft. One of the first things he did was to go down and see his Bank Manager, who greeted him genially, rather to his surprise. He was a new man since Edmund's day, very sleek and affable, with a bright flow of conversation about everything under the sun — except overdrafts. It was Edmund who first mentioned the beastly word. And Mr. Wayborough said hastily:

'Yes, yes. Most reluctant to press. Orders from Head Office, I'm afraid; nothing to do with my own feelings in the matter. However, all's well that ends well! I am so glad we were able to make little Mrs. Campion see that she would be well advised to sell. And considering that it has been rather neglected during the war — inevitably of course — I really think you were offered a very fair price for it. Yes.'

'For what?'

Mr. Wayborough looked taken aback.

'Surely . . . Do I understand? I was refer-ring to the sale of Hawkswood.' He glanced quickly away from Edmund's face. He said uneasily: 'You must have known.'

'I gave my wife power of attorney when I left England.'

'But, my dear sir, she must have cabled, she must have written you letters?' He said more hopefully, 'Very likely your mail was lost. A very likely thing to happen in the circumstances. How very distressing for you to learn of it so abruptly. And you have been home three days . . . Dear me!' he said in confusion. His sleek seal's face was agitated.

'Not at all. Please go on. Has the sale been concluded?'

'No! Oh, no! The conveyance has not yet been signed, I understand.'

It was easy enough to stop the sale. He had only to say he had changed his mind and withdraw the house from the market. But it was another matter to find a way of keeping it, a way of paying off its debts and earning enough to keep it going once again. Ah yes, that was a very different story. If now he had been married to Genevieve, she was so rich that running Hawkswood would be a bagatelle to her . . . He visualized the urgent repairs, the improvements and alterations that could be carried out with her money. It would be like damming a breach ... He visualized her in a ball dress, radiant, under the glittering chandeliers ... It was hard to keep her out of his thoughts in connection with Hawkswood. But he also was sternly practical. He began at once cutting down expenditure.

An obvious entrenchment was to dispense with all his unwanted guests. He said to Linda harshly:

'How much longer do these people intend to stay here? Do they think this is a charitable institution?'

She looked really shocked.

'Oh, Eddie, how unkind! And how unfair, besides! They're not living on charity; they all help with the expenses; they wouldn't want it otherwise. But even if they weren't paying, they *are* my family. You'd hardly call it charity to look after one's own family, would you?'

'Your family, they may be, but I fail to see why I should be obliged to keep them and cripple myself further.'

'But, Eddie — really how strange you are! — I've told you that they do contribute. Well — something, anyway.' When he stiffly inquired how much, she looked sulky and said: 'Daddy and Auntie Tory both give me twenty-five bob and the Hausers pay me thirty bob, which is absolutely all they can afford, poor lambs, and I only take it because it would humiliate them so to feel they were living on charity. Darling little Priscilla naturally can't pay, but I wouldn't expect her to; I look on her as one of my own children.'

Edmund felt again that painfully familiar sense of irritation. It was like arguing with a maddening child.

'It's very good of them to contribute so generously to the domestic exchequer, but all the same, Linda, I'm afraid you'll have to ask them to leave here.'

'I couldn't be so heartless,' she protested. 'Honestly, Eddie, I couldn't! What would become of them? Where would they go? Poor old things! Auntie Tory has only a small annuity, and Daddy — '

'Your father has quite a bit salted away, you can take my word for it. I know more about him than you think. He can well afford an establishment of his own, believe me. He can set up house with your aunt; and the Hausers can do a job of work.'

But Linda was so reluctant to turn them out that she made one excuse to herself after another, that the moment was not opportune (the sale of Hawkswood had been a different prospect — it would have been a year or more before they had to leave), and in this way several weeks slipped past with nothing said. It was fortunate that Edmund was not aware of this, but he had so much to attend to that he never bothered to inquire whether she had obeyed him. Besides, he scarcely troubled to speak to her unless he was obliged.

The fact was that he was beginning to realize that there was no way out of this mess for him — as things were. And even if he sold Hawkswood he would be no better off. The situation, then, was untenable; something had to be devised. His sense of futility, his distrust of life itself, made it seem an unreasonable task. He looked with a mounting sense of horror into the future, with Linda. It was not only that he had ceased to love her; he now bore her an active resentment. He would have liked to strike her, to knock her about really savagely as a punishment for her criminal stupidity. Of course that was impossible, but he elaborated the idea imaginatively as a sort of safety valve for his ill humor. He thought it was a piece of psychological cunning, on his part, to defraud himself. He had not the least suspicion of the danger inherent in this practice.

No, really Linda did not stand a chance from the beginning. Even if she had been faultless, one may doubt that the outcome would have been any different. It would be stupid to underrate Genevieve's influence on Edmund's desires just because for a year she had been only a memory. He wanted her: that was the point. It really did seem to him that if only he could marry Genevieve everything would be all right. Hawkswood restored . . . and Genevieve, the elusive, the mysterious, the desirable . . . Why, even life itself might take on some meaning then; or if that was too much to hope for, at least it would be more worth living than it was at present. He made up his mind and in his next letter to Genevieve he told her his intentions toward his wife.

He had been home nearly a fortnight when he went to Linda and told her he wanted a divorce.

She was sitting before her dressing table when he came in, and he saw the color flood into her face. He said quickly, to disabuse her mind of hope:

'I want to talk to you.'

She said ironically:

'Well, that will make a nice change!'

He put his hands in his pockets and said:

'Linda, I want you to divorce me.'

She went on mechanically smoothing the pad of cotton wool over her cheeks, along her forehead, and round her eyes, staring at her image in the glass, as if she had not heard. Indeed, in a sense she had not heard, for her mind had simply refused to accept the meaning of the words.

Into the silence he projected with an effort further words:

'I'm sorry it has to be like this. I know

it must come as something of a shock. But it's better to say a thing straight out than beat about the bush. You'd have to know sooner or later; we can't go on as we are, so much is obvious.'

'Oh, stop it! Stop it!' she cried, her face distorted, covering her ears. 'I won't listen to you! I don't know what you're talking about! You must be mad, coming here and talking like this to me!'

'Perhaps it was clumsy of me to blurt it out like that. I'm sorry. But it's no use running away from things because they're painful or unpleasant. One has to face facts. For God's sake let us discuss it calmly like rational beings.'

She dropped her trembling hands into her lap where he could not see them, and forced herself to speak calmly.

'Like rational beings? Suddenly, out of the blue, you come out with this terrible thing, something that's never entered my head, as coolly as if you were asking me to get you some new shirts. You're the one who is not being rational, believe me. And then you talk about sparing my feelings! Oh, my God! What do you think it feels like to have been married to a man for nearly ten years, to have borne him four children, and to be cast aside like — '

'For pity's sake,' said Edmund, closing his eyes, 'spare me the Lyceum rhetoric, I beg. Even people who have been married for ten years have been known to get a divorce when they were no longer happy living together.'

'According to you, marriage is no more significant than engaging a servant; you're on trial, and if you don't please, you can be dismissed, with alimony in lieu of a month's wages. I'm afraid it isn't quite as simple as that.' She gave him a strange little smile through the mirror; she looked white, queer, like a mad girl by Modigliani. 'Marriage is a sacrament. I will never divorce you.'

He said impatiently, paying no attention to her words but answering the tone of her voice: 'Why must you dramatize everything so? It's simply a matter of common sense and convenience. We don't get on well together — possibly we never did — and I've wasted so many years of my life that I think it would be sheer folly on my part to waste what is left to me.'

Her hands rearranged the bottles and brushes incessantly. It was hard to speak for the pain in her throat. She dragged out unsteadily:

'How long have you felt like this?'

'A long time now.'

Half to herself she said: 'I didn't know. I suppose I've been a blind fool.' And then to him: 'Is it because I let you down over the house? Is it because I have my family here?'

He said not unkindly:

'We can leave all that out of it, my dear. The reason I want my freedom is that I want to marry again. I met someone when I was in America during the war.' His tone became reminiscent, almost dreamy. 'We fell deeply in love,' he said huskily, as if he saw her there before him.

'I knew all along that you were infatuated with some woman. You gave yourself away when you couldn't bring yourself to touch me or kiss me.' She felt sick with the physical humiliation of being undesired.

'You see,' he said inanely, 'I love her in a way I've never loved you. It was one of those things — a *coup de foudre!* Neither of us could understand it. I've never felt like this for anyone else. And yet, she's not my type of person at all. Very beautiful. Very elusive. She's extraordinarily honest, too, and yet it's not a bit your sort of honesty that one can see through to the very bottom, like clear water. With all her frankness, she is still maddeningly elusive, terribly exciting — '

She sprang up, knocking some of the toilet things off the table in her agitation, unheeded. She spun round and stared directly at him for the first time, with eyes like shrill blue pebbles in her frantic face.

'Shut up!' she cried in a high voice. 'Shut up! Shut up! I don't want to hear. How dare you tell me about your filthy amours! You must be mad . . . Oh! Oh! Oh! It's like a nightmare! Mother of God, I think I'm going mad myself,' she sobbed, holding her temples with both hands and rocking painfully back and forth.

Edmund stared at her in amazement. This neurotic agitation of hers, so ill-judged and unseemly, was in such sharp contrast with his Genevieve's exquisite unruffled

118

poise and dignity that he could not help feeling disgusted by his wife with a kind of weak contemptuous pity.

'For God's sake, don't cry!' he implored pettishly. 'You know I can't bear tears. Whose fault is it if I don't love you anymore? It's just one of those things, my dear girl. Can't you see that we've grown so far apart that we could never live together again ... ? Leaving Genevieve out of it.'

'It's no use discussing it,' she said harshly, drying her eyes, composing her face. 'I will never divorce you!'

'You can't say that!' he protested.

'I will never divorce you,' she repeated. 'I will never divorce you.'

When he had gone, she sat staring at the closed door. She repeated over and over to herself like an hypnotic: It's an infatuation, nothing more than an infatuation. He'll come back to me if I don't lose my head. They always do. They always go back to their wives in the end. The wife holds all the cards, they say. I only have to play them properly. And the children make it even more certain; he'd never leave them. I have done my duty. I don't see that he has anything to reproach me with. It's not my fault that everything went wrong while he was away. And I must be careful not to reproach him either. I must be very tactful, very patient. I'll be sweet to him, very sweet. I won't think about *her*. I'll take more pains with my appearance, I really will. I'll get my hair set every week, and wear stockings, and get my nails manicured. I'll *make* him take an interest in me again . . . On and on into the sleepless dawn she plotted her hopeless little plans.

But she had little chance to put her plans into execution, for the very next day Edmund received a cablegram. He seemed to take a very long time to read its message, staring down at the flimsy slip of paper with an unfathomable expression.

'Well?' demanded Great-Aunt Tory, as inquisitive as a child, tapping her knife with restless impatience against her plate. 'Is it bad news?' The older we get the more desirable is bad news — for somebody else.

Edmund folded the paper quickly and

put it in his pocket.

'Thank you, no. I have to go to London for a few days,' he said curtly.

Linda's eyes were fastened on him, with all her heart showing anxiously in them. She said timidly:

'Shall you be back for Oliver's birthday?'

'I've no idea.'

★ ★ ★

Genevieve had purposely told him to meet her in London — not Southampton. She did not want to be caught at a disadvantage, looking even ever so slightly less than her exquisite best. She preferred to fight the arduous battle with the Customs alone, with no uneasy consciousness of a stray lock of hair, a smudged lipstick, a creased shirtwaist, being regarded with a critical eye. Only her own critical demand for perfection could imagine Edmund or any man seeing flaws in her appearance, especially at such a moment. But for her the moment was all-important; first impressions counted for so much. And this was almost a first impression. She would not for the world have him disillusioned. Any disappointment there was to be must be hers; she had made up her mind to that. And if she was satisfied, all would be well.

She had brought her car with her, and she drove fast on the unfamiliar road to London. A room was reserved for her at the Ritz Hotel. Edmund's club was conveniently near in Dover Street. They were going to have a wonderful time! Of course Edmund found her more desirable than ever. Because now she was desirable in rather a different way. It was partly the old enchantment of her mysterious femininity, her gentle unshakable confidence that what she wanted would be — the sublime confidence, in effect, of a fabulously rich person who has never known defeat and who therefore does not believe in its existence. That attitude to life has a powerful fascination on those for whom defeat sits always like a spider in the corner of the room.

Then it would seem to Edmund that this exquisite refinement and particularity was symbolical of her mind and character.

Looking at the jewels weighing down her slender wrists, the jewels against her neck, he could not forget her wealth, all her suave life . . . He would think of his debts, he would think of Hawkswood, and then he would think: If I could marry her . . . Staring at her, like a child gazing through a confectioner's plate-glass window, with all his hungry soul in his eyes.

'Stop looking as if you're going to eat me, darling, for goodness sake, or they'll send for the manager,' she laughed softly, very well pleased with her effect on him. The funny little man! What she saw in him she couldn't imagine. He was not beautiful or gay; he was not a type she admired and had none of the qualities she looked for in a man. He wasn't even gentle and sweet, like Paul. But that iron-controlled physiognomy hinting at rigidly repressed emotion never failed to stir her pulses, quicken her heart beats. He was a man who looked capable of anything, and the notion, with its threat of cruelty, excited her.

That first evening they were too happy in each other's presence to talk of the future. She did not mention marriage, and so Edmund had no need to mention to her the sour word 'divorce.' They had a champagne supper to celebrate their reunion, and then they drove round the park dreamily in the light summer dusk. It was in that tricky light betwixt and between, and she leaned against his shoulder as she drove. She must have turned her head momentarily toward him, or been fooled by the shadows, for suddenly there was a cry and the car jerked, under Edmund's hands, askew and then to a standstill.

'My God! What was that?' said Genevieve faintly. 'Have I run into something? I felt a bump.'

'It looked to me as if he fell in front of the car,' said Edmund swinging open the door.

'Lordy, lordy! Have I killed him?' said Genevieve, closing her eyes tightly and clinging to the steering wheel as if it was a life belt.

'I'm going to see. Wait there!'

Edmund called: 'It's all right. No damage done. Only shaken. We'll drive him home. Help me get him in the front, dear, it's easier. I'll sit at the back, unless you'd like me to drive.'

'No, it's all right,' Genevieve said softly, eyeing her victim apologetically.

He was tall, absurdly handsome, with a quizzical eyebrow and a helpless smile; he stood there smiling at Genevieve as if he'd come to a party.

Edmund said: 'My dear chap, do bend! You can't hope to get in unless you bend.'

'Extraordinarily kind of you,' he commented gratefully, bending his head but forgetting to raise his feet, and in consequence nearly falling on his nose.

Drunk, mouthed Edmund silently over his head.

'Drunk!' said the man, and giggled boyishly. He leaned back in the seat and flicked back his silver locks. He said with convincing gravity: 'Remarkably lucky thing I happened to be drunk tonight; otherwise I might have been killed. Fatal to be knocked down if you're not drunk. Advise everybody to get drunk if they're going to be run over.'

'It's charming of you to take it like that,' said Genevieve. 'Where shall I drive you?'

Edmund from the back suggested that they ought to take him to a doctor just to make sure no unknown damage had been done.

'I'm a doctor,' he assured them. 'A very special specialist from Harley Street.' He made it sound like a line from a comic song. His name was Dr. Paul. He said: 'Can we go and have a drink somewhere? I want to tell you the story of my life.' He was inconsequential and absurd.

There was a streak of mud on his cheek and Genevieve leaned forward to brush it gently away. He looked up at her fixedly with a peculiar expression of intensity.

'Now,' said Dr. Paul indulgently, 'I will tell you the story of my life . . . ' They were feeling so good-humored that his absurdities only amused them. Presently he leaned forward to whisper in Genevieve's ear: 'Can't we get rid of this chap? I want to be alone with you. I feel this is a terribly important moment in both our lives, no other person should profane it by being present. I should like it to be — ' he made a beautiful gesture — 'quite — quite sacred.'

'That would be nice. But I don't think it would be quite kind to him, you know.'

Dr. Paul said confidentially: 'Let's shake off this fellow! I know a place much more amusing than this where they have some really drinkable whisky.'

'It's sweet of you, but I couldn't do that.'

'You could do anything, you're so beautiful. You don't mind me saying that you're beautiful, do you? Because you are, and I don't like to see you going around with a type like this. I don't like him. Do you?'

'Well, yes, I do.'

Dr. Paul turned round and peered at Edmund curiously.

'Do you? Why?' he asked.

'I suppose I'm used to him,' said Genevieve lightly.

'You're not going to tell me he's your husband,' he said suspiciously.

'Well — not exactly. Not yet,' said Genevieve.

'Not yet? Not yet?' he grumbled. 'That's a fine thing to tell me after nearly running me over. How do you think that makes me feel?'

They turned into Harley Street.

'Come on, this is where you live,' said Edmund. 'What number do you want?'

'Dear old man, the best of pals,' said Dr. Paul affectionately. 'I'll take whatever number you give me . . . Double or quits, eh?'

He smiled at them charmingly. He got out of the car.

A slightly unreal expression fixed his features. He said very formally: 'Thank you so much for a perfectly delightful evening.'

They watched him stalk up the moonlit steps with the deliberateness of a heron and disappear into the house without a backward glance.

6

A couple of days later Edmund drove her in the Packard down to Hawkswood. It looked its loveliest just then at the beginning of June and she was enchanted with what she saw of it, which was not much — glimpses caught through the trees.

She said: 'No wonder you don't want to give it up!'

He looked at her gratefully — 'as kind as she was fair!' — it was wonderful to have someone who could understand without a lot of labored explanations how you felt about the important things in your life. Since she was rich she understood money very well. He described his financial predicament to her and she listened seriously and sensibly and sometimes put her finger acutely on a point.

'But,' she said, without any unnatural pride or self-consciousness, 'it will be all right soon, when we are married. And meanwhile we can make some arrangement. I'll get my lawyer to fix it.'

He said: 'I wish it was all as simple as you make it sound. It's not going to be so easy.' He hesitated. 'You'll have to know sometime.' He looked at her crossly, as though it was somehow her fault. 'Linda won't divorce me.'

'She won't divorce you?' she repeated incredulously. 'But why not?'

'Oh, she doesn't believe in divorce,' he shrugged.

'Doesn't believe in it?' echoed Genevieve again. 'I've never heard of such a thing! One might as well say one doesn't believe in income tax, it seems to me. Did you tell her about us — about me?'

'Of course.'

'Well, then?'

'Well, nothing. It doesn't make a particle of difference to her; except that I suppose she rationalizes it to herself as a mere infatuation that I shall get over if only she hangs on like grim death and performs all those sickeningly futile little rites that women go through at such a time.'

'But, Edmund, surely you've explained — '

'My dear girl, you can have no idea what it means to explain *anything* to Linda. She has the silly obstinate mind of a child, and the strength of her prejudices is irresistible. It's like battering one's head against a wall; at the end of an argument with her one comes away bruised and bleeding, having gained nothing. She simply shuts her mind to whatever you may say. She is perverse and unalterable and mean.'

Still, when he left her that night, he murmured against her cheek: 'Don't leave me! . . . Don't leave me just yet, honey! Give me time! I'll think of a solution. Every problem has its answer.'

Genevieve, too, hoped that with patience Linda might change her mind. And because she wanted to be alone with Edmund, undisturbed, she began looking for a suitable furnished flat. She knew exactly what she wanted, and she was lucky enough to find it quite quickly in Brook Street: a top-floor flat from the windows of which she could see the treetops waving in Grosvenor Square. It had charm and distinction.

It would make an agreeable setting for her. It's most desirable feature for Genevieve was that no one else lived in the house. There was an alarmingly expensive antique shop at street level; above that there was a Russian milliner who made wonderful little hats and had her showroom on one floor and her workroom above it. Then the top floor.

Edmund could come and go unobserved, and stay the night, with no one the wiser. That seemed to her fair enough. That did not seem to her deceitful but merely discreet. With Quaker propriety, she valued her good name above everything.

She took the flat without hesitation for a period of three months with a monthly option thereafter. She was even lucky enough, or wealthy enough, to find the perfect maid, capable, discreet, and, even at such short notice, devotedly loyal. That was early in July.

It happened also about this time that Edmund ran into Ivor Campion, his cousin, and took him down to Hawkswood to stay. Edmund said:

'Look after him, Linda. He's had a rotten time. Make him feel at home; let him feel he's welcome to stay as long as he likes.'

Linda said: 'Aren't you staying, then?'

'A night or two, just to settle him in. Then I have business to attend to.'

'Yes, of course,' she agreed in a small docile voice, but could not forbear to add: 'Only I never see anything of you now.'

He looked impatient.

'What do you want to see me about?'

She said: 'Oh, Eddie!' and covered her face with her hands so that he should not see and be irritated by the quick-springing tears.

He drew in his breath. But after a moment or two he said, kindly enough: 'Come and walk round the place with me. Has Strivens relayered the hedge on the east side of South Field where Newton's cows broke through?'

And before he left he again commended Ivor to her care.

'Be nice to him,' he said.

Edmund and his cousin had never been on noticeable terms of intimacy in the old days before the war, for the obvious reason that there was nearly ten years' difference between them. But during the war they chanced to land themselves in the same prisoner-of-war camp for a few months. That experience created a certain relationship between them to which the blood-tie contributed not a little. Then Edmund contrived, with three others, to escape; and Ivor was transferred to another camp. Four years of Ivor's war had been spent in the excruciating idleness of a prison camp. He came out looking at least twelve years older than his real age, which was twenty-seven, hollow-eyes, skeletal, and pathetically sunburnt. It was his good fortune to run into Edmund just after receiving his discharge from the military convalescent home where he had been fitted with his new foot. He was only too glad to accept Edmund's invitation. He had no home. There was no one to look after him, no one to care a row of pins for him, if it came to that — not that he cared. He was glad that he had no family to fuss over him; he had a kind of grim confidence in himself.

He had, as yet, not the faintest notion how he meant to earn his living. He had no job, no prospects, no career even, for he had still been at Cambridge when war broke out. For hours in the convalescent home he languidly buttered through career-guidance pamphlets. He found it surprisingly difficult to decide anything. Not that that agitated him. For twenty-seven years he had not had to make any attempt to keep himself, so that he could not wholly adjust himself to the idea now. He had his gratuity and his pension; there was no need to decide anything until he had built himself up again. He was inclined to be neurotically preoccupied about his diet, at present. He still weighed under eight stone. It would be quite permissible to loaf for a few months in the country on the pretext of writing a book about his war experiences.

Ivor's presence revived all kinds of memories in Werner. He had some knowledge of what it meant to be a prisoner: he had been three weeks in Buchenwald, five months in Dachau. There was little he had not experienced of that sort of torture.

'That would have been worse than anything I went through,' said Ivor.

'Indeed, yes,' Werner agreed. He held up bunches of his hair: 'I came out of Dachau with all these white hairs. Isn't it, Ilse? Ask Ilse, she will tell you what I was like. A ruin. I weighed forty-two kilos only. Imagine that!'

They imagined.

When Ivor volunteered, quite eagerly, to help Linda with the washing-up or whatever happened to be the chore of the moment (Miss Sharpe smiled on him when she heard this, with all her usual unreliable benignity: 'Delighted to hear you mean to do something to earn your keep, young man. Quite enough parasites living here as it is.' Ivor bowed to her charmingly and said: 'But we don't expect old people to work'), Linda accepted. She was obliged to; it was not that she liked to have him limping at her heels while she performed her necessary tiresome tasks but, having promised Edmund to give him her special attention, she was far too conscientious not to carry it out. Anyway, it was agreeable enough for a few days to listen to some words of praise about herself. And Ivor was nice, she found, not in the least frightening.

She let him talk to her for hours of his experiences. And once in the garden after one of these conversations he kissed her. Although the kiss was harmless enough, she was very cross at this 'silly behavior,' and would not address a word to him all the next day. He was obliged to write her a letter of apology and explanation. Of course she was bound to forgive eventually, and even to forget what happened.

Once Ilse said to her:

'Ivor becomes quite good-looking, I think.'

'Does he?' said Linda. 'I haven't noticed.'

'No?' Ilse said, smiling. 'And you are together so much. I find that very unobservant of you, my dear.'

So that the next time she was with Ivor she did observe him, and not with her usual absent look.

'Yes,' she said, 'I believe you are putting on weight. Ilse said you were. At least, she said you were getting quite nice-looking, which I suppose is the same thing.'

'I certainly feel much better. I suppose I shall have to go out into the heartless world again soon and find a job.'

'Oh, nonsense!'

Ivor said: 'No, I do think I'm taking advantage of your kindness. It isn't right. I don't think Edmund has any idea of how much you have to do, how much you have to carry on those thin little shoulders. Somebody ought to nurse you into putting on a bit more weight, my dear; you're like a wraith. You seem to get thinner and whiter every day.'

'Oh, Ivor, how absurd you are! You talk as if I was going into a genteel decline, instead of merely being rather overworked like every other housewife in England today.'

'I wonder what Edmund would say if he saw you.'

'I doubt if he'd notice. He knows I'm very strong.'

'You speak as though you thought Edmund didn't care.'

'Do I?' She leaned her forehead against the pane and stared out into the garden.

'I'd better go and say good night to the children. They won't go to sleep till I do.'

Ivor very lightly clasped her shoulders. He said gently:

'My dear, won't you tell me what the trouble is?'

'Trouble?' she said in a high-strained voice. 'There's no trouble. What should there be?'

'Do you think I can't see your unhappiness? Do you think I haven't seen the tears forcing themselves past your eyelids sometimes when you think no one is looking? My heart aches for you.'

'Oh, don't, Ivor . . . Please . . . Please! I don't know what you're talking about . . . I must go!'

'You are so desperately loyal. I love it in you.'

The words 'desperately loyal' for some reason nearly choked her with sobs. She found herself crying against his shoulder. His arms were round her comfortingly and he made comforting noises. She took his handkerchief and dried her eyes quite vigorously.

'If Ilse had come in just then, I don't

know what she'd have thought. She's already told me that I see too much of you. I suppose she thinks it isn't respectable.'

'Never mind that,' he said quickly.

'No, I must go, Ivor. It was just a moment's foolishness. I expect I'm tired. Forgive me! And — please — say no more about it.' She gave him a fleeting tear-stained smile and was gone like a little ghost in a shabby blue cotton frock.

There was no need for Ivor to go against her expressed wishes by talking of it again: she spoke of it herself. She thought to herself that she would never mention it again, she honestly intended not to — she was, as Ivor said, desperately loyal; nevertheless, her heart was breaking with what she should do. If she had had a mother . . . if there had been someone for her to confide in . . . But there was no one. Even Nanny Potter, whose warm proverbial wisdom would have been a comfort, she dared not speak to, not from shame of mentioning such private matters of the heart to a member of the 'lower orders,' but simply because she knew that all Nanny Potter's loyalties were with Edmund and it was not very likely that, in nursery parlance, she would listen to tales against her very favorite.

So Ivor said nothing more, was almost indecently uninquisitive you might have said. And a couple of days later, her eyes intent on the porridge she was flopping into the children's bowls, she said carelessly:

'Did you know that Edmund was in love with someone else?'

'So that's what the trouble is! Did he tell you?'

'He expects me to divorce him.'

'He wants to marry the other woman, is that the idea?'

But one cannot speak of emotional matters so early in the morning, let alone that there was the breakfast to get and serve. She found herself at her tasks for the rest of the day mentally engaging in long heart-rending conversations with him, conversations in which, curiously enough, he said practically nothing but was an Aeolian harp responding to the wind of her eloquence. For once she was actually eager to get him alone. She was aware of Ilse's raised eyebrows when she invited him to come for a walk with her that evening.

They walked in silence for a little way. Then Ivor said:

'I've been thinking all day of what you told me.'

With that opening, she could plunge right in.

' . . . some horrible American girl he's picked up. You know what they're like, Ivor. He'll be sick of her in three months. As a matter of fact, I don't suppose he really means to marry her at all. I think it's just that he's tired of me and wants to be free. As though that was all there is to marriage! That's what I tried to explain to him, but he won't listen, he won't believe me. He's like a horrible stubborn child — just stands there with a wooden face and shuts his ears to everything you're saying, till your head feels quite bruised and bleeding from banging it against the stone wall of his mind.' She put her hands to her temples, as though they really were bruised.

Ivor murmured that he did sound unreasonable.

'Could we sit down on this wall a little? You're racing along so fast, I can't keep up.'

She stopped, relaxed, and even laughed a little, guiltily.

'My poor Ivor! How patient you have been to listen to this long tedious complaint. This is how all wives go on, I suppose, when they've been married ten years.' She gave a dry little unamused laugh. 'I never thought I should be one of them; I really did believe what they told me about love lasting forever. Isn't it absurd? I thought it was my love and all my prayers that brought Edmund safely through the war; but if it was only for another woman, it wasn't worthwhile.

'Why did God bring him back, if I'm not meant to have him anymore? I'd rather he was dead; then at least I shouldn't have lost him; he would still be mine.' She crossed herself rapidly. 'I didn't mean that,' she said. She said in a low humble voice: 'I'm very self-willed, I know. I ought to make a willing sacrifice of my feelings. But I can't! I can't! I don't believe I'm meant to give him up to God. Or why did God give him to me in the first place, in marriage? Marriage is a sacrament and can never be revoked. Marriage is only ended in death.'

So that was the way she felt about it, he thought.

Particularly not looking at her, he asked:

'Do you love him?'

'Why, of course I do,' she said, and laughed.

'No, no. This is just between you and me. I don't want to know what you consider the appropriate emotion, but what you really do feel in that funny little heart of yours.'

'Why, you donkey, of course I love him! Haven't you understood a word of all I've been saying?'

'All right,' he said. 'I'm sorry! Let's go back now, shall we?'

'Why are you so nice to me, I wonder?'

He looked down at her with a wry smile.

'Nice to you? Because I give you a little

of the consideration and sympathy you need? You don't ask for very much from life, do you? And there's that great houseful of people for whom you slave your fingers to the bone — '

'Oh, hush!' She put her fingers to his lips and he caught and held them. 'You mustn't say anything against them. I couldn't speak to my own family. You wouldn't expect it. But, oh! Ivor, it has been such a relief to tell someone at last. You've no idea!'

He looked at her whimsically: 'One day I'll tell you my secret,' he said.

But she did not raise her head, only continued to flatten and stroke the lapel of his coat, as though she had not heard. She whispered something; then cleared her throat and asked timidly, with painful hopefulness:

'Ivor! Do you think he'll ever come back to me?'

* * *

From her bedroom window Ilse had chanced to see their return, as they stood in the drive with Linda fingering his lapel shyly and Ivor gazing down at the top of her head, his expression invisible, Ilse was very roguish to him about it. But, queerly, he made no response — only looked at her ironically with quirked brows. She gazed back insolently. A slow reluctant smile curled the corners of Ivor's mouth. Ilse's lips parted slightly, like a hungry flower. She might have been about to speak; but she said nothing.

Ivor said: 'It must be very dull for you here, day in, day out. Do you never go to London?'

'I could go to London if I wished,' Ilse replied languidly. 'If there was anything to go for.'

Ivor grinned suddenly and, turning, limped away.

At supper that night he remarked casually that he was going up to town on the following day. Linda looked disappointed.

'You never told me,' she said stupidly.

'Now what am I supposed to reply to that accusation?' asked Ivor good-humoredly.

Ilse said: 'I, too, should be going to

London. I am needing to visit my dentist. I have a tooth here — '

She opened her mouth wide and groped an indicative finger at the back somewhere.

He and Ilse traveled up on different trains but met in the immense palm-fringed and rococo lobby of the Universal Palace. She had an amber-filled glass beside her. She glanced up at him casually when he appeared, with no change of expression, with no word of greeting.

He said pleasantly: 'It was nice of you to come. I was half afraid you might change your mind at the last moment.'

'I always do what I want to do,' she said, giving him a slow somber glance.

'My word, do you really?' Ivor said, pretending to be impressed. 'I do admire people who manage to do that.'

'Also,' she said coolly, 'you must not take me for a fool. I understand more than you think, perhaps. And I am very, very discreet. You need have nothing to fear.'

Ivor said: 'You know, I don't believe we're talking of the same thing. Or are we?' Her eyes met his and held them.

'Oh, yes, I see we are!' He smiled mischievously.

She said huskily: 'You have a very beautiful mouth . . . '

★ ★ ★

. . . Her hair lay across his face. She stirred in his arms and remarked:

'I suppose you think me very wicked to Werner.'

His arm tightened round her obligingly.

'My pretty *Katzchen*, don't let us spoil a delightful moment by such considerations.'

She pinched him hard.

'Little beast!'

'I want you should understand that I take from Werner nothing that is any longer his. At Dauchau, you understand, they have done such things to him . . . '

'Look, *Katzchen* darling, it isn't terribly tactful of you to tell me these things about your husband. It makes me feel uncomfortable, guilty; not a nice thing to do. I'd rather hear that he was cruel to you, beat you, or simply that you no longer loved him.'

'But of course I love him. What are you thinking? That I love you, you — you — creature, you?'

Ivor laughed and pulled her face down to his.

'No, no, I can tell you don't!'

Between kisses he added, laughing: 'And what's more. I don't care a fig for you either!'

'Oh, no,' she purred contentedly in his arms. 'We all know who is a fig for you, though.'

'Do tell!'

'Do I have to tell you who you are in love with? It gives me great pleasure to think of it,' she avowed, lying against him like a huge voluptuous cat. She began to quiver with wicked mirth. 'It is the good little mousy Linda! Who you will never get, I think. She is much too honorable. Ha, Ha! Poor Ivor!'

7

Now Linda had someone to confide in, and confide she did. She was never alone with this much-to-be-pitied Ivor without immediately plunging back into these sad seas wherein her mind eddied wretchedly round and round to the point of foundering. Ivor was quite remarkably patient.

She was endeavoring now to take more pains with her appearance. She usually remembered at least to dash some powder on her face and run a lipstick — though it was perhaps rather too garish a red — over her mouth. Often she managed to get her hair set, and she bought herself a highly unsuitable dress in the altogether vain hope that Edmund would find her more interesting if she changed her style and became more sophisticated, as she imagined the American girl to be. She had the idea that she should compete with her on her own ground.

As it happened, on the rare occasions

when Edmund came down, it was not to stay — a mere rushed few hours, for one purpose or another, generally business, and either she forgot to put the dress on, or if she did he didn't notice it. With her bare legs and sandals, she only succeeded in looking like a girl dressed up when she did wear the frock. She never could remember to wear stockings, for they only got ripped into holes in the garden or split with a sudden crack when she knelt to her domestic chores, and, 'one simply couldn't afford the coupons,' she said. Her little ruined hands were red and their nails hopelessly bitten still. Really she looked better when she didn't try so hard, and was just her simple take-it-or-leave-it self. However, Ivor said nothing to dishearten her, and she was not entirely unaware of the way his eyes rested on her. She found it not unpleasing. Yet she was wholeheartedly shocked and furious when he kissed her.

It happened one evening when Ivor had been more than usually sympathetic and she had been wrought to the point of tears, a passion of weeping for Edmund, when suddenly Ivor lifted her face, tear-stained and forlorn, and with calm decisiveness kissed her parted lips in a manner that could hardly be mistaken by the most innocent for the chaste kiss of pure affection. Not till he chose to let her go could she express her outrage. She put her fist to her mouth, her eyes large with horror.

'You beast! . . . How could you?' she cried in sincere dismay.

'Do you think I'm made of stone? Here you weep, almost in my arms. I should be less than human if I didn't want to comfort you.'

'You weren't trying to comfort me, you loathsome beast! Don't make it worse by lying.'

'Very well, then. I was trying to comfort myself. What do you think it's like for me day after day, listening to you talk all the time about another man, seeing you so miserable, and being so helpless? Have you ever given it a thought? You know I'm madly in love with you, don't you?'

'Of course I didn't. You oughtn't to talk to me like this,' she said unsteadily.

'Why not?' he said boldly. 'Why shouldn't you hear of someone else's unhappiness for a change? You think I've taken advantage of you by kissing you just now, but, believe me, it's nothing compared with the advantage you've taken of me day after day, playing on my feelings.'

She stared.

'I don't understand. And I think it's dreadful of you to speak like this. I don't know how you dare, when you're Edmund's friend!'

'Is it any worse than the things his wife has said about him?'

'You must be mad! I won't listen to you,' she said, and ran away.

They were excruciatingly civil to one another for the next few days when they had occasion to address a remark in public, but when they were alone each preserved a rigid silence toward the other.

Presently, as Ivor had foreseen, because of Linda's failure with Edmund and consequent loss of self-confidence, there arose in her queer little heart inexplicable feelings that she had been the one to behave badly to Ivor, that she had been unfair, that she was guilty of meanness and unwitting cruelty to him even. His quiet disdain and persevering silence convinced her more than any words and protestations could have done that he was in the right.

On the fourth day after the 'quarrel,' she said to him shyly when she found him alone (he no longer helped her about the house, of course, and she had scarcely seen him these last days):

'Don't you think we could be friends again?'

His dark saturnine face was unsmiling, his eyes cold. For the first time it occurred to her with something of a shock that he had a cruel face, that he could be more heartless, more ruthless than Edmund. She was aware of her heartbeats, uneasy with fear.

He said, so severely that it was a moment or two before she took in his meaning:

'How can we be friends? My feelings about you are unchanged.'

She stammered:

'Well . . . then . . . I — '

'I think it will be best for me if I go away. If I don't see you, sooner or later I shall forget you.'

She brought out a laugh, a little shakily.

'Well, I don't call that a very pretty speech, I must say.'

His unsmiling look accused her of flippancy. She stared at him. Hardly moving his lips, he said:

'You do not know the pain in my heart.'

She felt ashamed, and a tenderness of romantic pity welled up in her own heart for him. Ah, did she not know the anguish of unrequited love! Besides, she could not afford to throw away so flattering a balm. And somewhere, in the very depths of her darkest consciousness flickered a tiny revengeful notion that here was someone who could be made to suffer as Edmund was making her suffer.

She said, low:

'You are the only friend I've got. There's no one else I can talk to here. I don't know what I shall do without you.'

'I'll do whatever you want,' he said deeply, his expression softening. He took her small rough hands in his.

She bent her head so that he could hardly catch the words.

'I want you to stay.'

'Then I'll stay,' he said, and slid his hands up her arms.

'Yes, but Ivor — ' She drew back. How was she to word it without upsetting him again?

But he understood. He reassured her a little mockingly.

'I promise I'll behave,' he said.

That night he slipped a letter under her door, describing his misery of the last few days after that 'ungovernable impulse' as he called the kiss, describing his love and his devotion, etc. Thereafter she received many letters from him. It would be foolish to pretend they displeased her. She thought it was wrong of him to write them and dishonorable of herself to read them. To her way of thinking, Edmund's infidelity did not excuse it. Nevertheless, she did read the letters, and what is more, could not quite bring herself to destroy these testimonials to her charm and adorability. She used to toss them furtively into the false bottom of an old converted workbox, in which she kept other 'important' papers for which she could find no place in her daily life.

Yet, despite all his wiles, she granted him nothing. Not one embrace, not a touch of the hand nor even a caressing word. She was scrupulously honest with him.

She would say not one word more than she meant; and in her affections she was adamantly faithful to Edmund.

It infuriated Ivor.

'How can you be so stupid?' he stormed at her. 'Don't you know that he despises your virtue, he doesn't want it, he'd like you the more for knowing you were no better than himself. I can tell you, no man likes a woman to be his superior, morally or in any other way. Don't you know that virtue and chastity are no longer *de rigueur*, you obstinate girl?'

'But I love him,' she explained pitifully.

'Who's talking about love, you silly little thing? Why can't you enjoy yourself, without bringing love into it? You don't have to be thirsty before you can enjoy a glass of wine, do you? You think I'm a pagan, but let me tell you, I worship God through the gratification of my senses, as He meant me to. Or why did He give them to me? Wake up, you maddening little medieval creature, this isn't the Dark Ages!'

'They seem like the Dark Ages to me,' she said simply. 'I don't see that they could be much darker.'

The affair between Ilse and Ivor continued cordial. They managed to contrive many little opportunities for their pleasure. They were both so deft, so expert, that they had no fear of anyone's finding out. Not even the keenest eye could catch a glance between them, or unravel a hint from a sentence addressed ostensibly to someone else. Neither was so obtuse as to look up or flush with desire when the other entered the room. Yet this man who was perfectly controlled in public where Ilse was concerned was the same man who openly languished after Linda, standing near her, following her with his eyes on all occasions, restless till he could get her alone, obviously troubled if he chanced to touch her. And even Linda was noticeably inclined to rest her eyes on him sometimes with a puzzled expression; she paid far more attention to him than Ilse did.

All the same, Werner knew.

Edmund had been down for a couple of days. At first he had been sweet, had taken the children to a fair in the neighborhood, and been not disagreeable about the house. All sorts of mad hopes flew into Linda's heart. If only he'd come back, she prayed, and vowed special vows to her five favorite saints and particularly to her best of all, the Little Flower, Saint Thérèse. But before her avowed intentions could reach heaven, her bright dreams were broken by Edmund's renewing his plea to be divorced. That, it appeared, was the reason for his pleasant visit, hoping that sweetness would prevail where argument had proved useless. But, 'Never, never!' cried Linda, the tears falling through her fingers. So after all it ended in a row.

But it left her with the determination to use her own energies more spiritedly. She had not tried hard enough to please him. For instance, he had asked her to get rid of her 'paying' guests, and she had deliberately ignored it. No wonder he was angry and hated her. They should all go, and when Hawkswood was empty once more perhaps his desire to be back in it would return.

She shrank from Great-Aunt Tory's vicious tongue and she dreaded her father's ignoble appeals; it seemed therefore easiest to begin with the Hausers. She would explain it to Werner Hauser. She always found it easier to talk to a man than a woman. Werner was gentleness itself, he would not make it difficult for her. At the worst, he would only make her feel a little sad and uncomfortable.

' . . . It is my husband, you see,' she said earnestly, twisting her fingers.

'Yes, I see,' Werner said dully.

'If I had only myself to consider I'd be glad for you to stay as long as you might wish. But, you see, Edmund feels — He has plans . . . I do wish you'd sit down, Mr. Werner.'

'Thank you, I am all right. It was so

good of you to bear us for such a long time. Much kindness you have given us. It is quite right you should tell us when we are no longer agreeable to you.' He rested one long sensitive hand on the table to stop its trembling.

'Please don't say things like that. It isn't that we don't want you — '

Werner's sad dark eyes flickered up for an instant, piercing her with a glance of such despair that it frightened her. He said at once with his exquisite politeness, however:

'I perfectly comprehend. I shall explain to Ilse. I am sure she will understand. We shall leave at once. We would not wish you to be inconvenienced after so much kindness.'

'Please,' said Linda. 'There's no hurry for two or three days . . . '

Werner bowed.

It was naturally something he wished to tell his wife right away. It was an undeniable blow. There were plans to be made. Ilse would be very gay and optimistic about it, and she would conjure instantly a whole flock of brilliant new ideas out of her brain, to inspire him with courage. She had this altogether amazing faculty of turning disaster into a triumph. He was tender, neurotic, pessimistic death-absorbed, with a profound distrust of experience — the direct opposite, in his attitude toward life, of his wife, Ilse. So that now, as he climbed the stairs, he longed for her reassurance and strength.

The door of their bedroom was locked.

His fingers were suddenly too slippery to turn the handle. He stood there at attention, his shoulders bowed, keeping himself upright by leaning his forehead ever so lightly against the door.

He fancied he could hear a torment whispering within. His face took on lines of agonizing strain . . .

Exactly so had he once stood outside the drawing room of their flat in the Lindenstrasse, trying to open a door that was locked.

He had gone down into the lobby and had rung their flat on the telephone, and then, leaving the receiver off, had run back up stairs and listened to it ringing,

ringing, ringing, because she dared not answer it. It gave him a sour feeling of triumph to think how it must have agitated them, that insistent, wild ringing. He never found out which of their friends shared his drawing room and his wife on that occasion. They had been married about two years. So far as he knew it was the only time she had been unfaithful to him. And he left her then for several months, during which time he produced a scholarly and delicately inspired little volume on Fleme. After its small but gratifying success, they somehow came together again.

If it had not been so, he would probably never have got out of Dachau alive. He owed that to his wife, just as he owed it to her that they were able to leave Austria and the Third Reich not entirely destitute. There was a certain Nazi official for whom she was able to render some small services not un-divorced from her personal charms. This it was inevitable that Werner should discover on his release. That he owed his freedom to his wife on such terms somehow did more to

163

break his spirit than all the humiliations and pains inflicted on him by the Nazis in the camp.

'But all that was only for you, my darling,' she swore. 'And now we shall put all that behind us and start a new life abroad.'

He knew that he was no longer able to satisfy her, but this new affront to his manhood sickened him afresh, as though it had never occurred before. He did not bother to wonder who it was with her behind that shamefully locked door; he only felt a childish crumbling anger that she should fail him at the very moment when he most required her sustenance.

'Ilse!' he called softly twice, and waited. 'Ilse!' he cried, and rapped sharp knuckles on the door. 'Ilse, are you awake?' He shook the door. Aware of the absurdity of standing there shouting: 'Let me in, Ilse! Let me in!' yet with a dour obstinacy he continued, till he imagined their stifled laughter . . . voluptuous hysteria . . . His hands fell to his sides. He walked away down the passage with the stiff gait of a sailor or a blind man . . .

That evening, playing double dummy with Miss Sharpe, his eyes never raised from the cards, he became aware that his wife's lover was Ivor Campion.

In a sudden flash of intuition — or self-torturing invention — he thought, she'd like to marry him. He's young and doubtless pleasing to a woman like Ilse. And if she married him she'd be English and safe. Nothing to worry about any more. She'd have a home.

It was then that his own desire for 'home' overpowered him. He felt a voluptuous weariness enwrap him, into which he aspired to sink forever.

It distracted his mind from the humiliation outside the bedroom to think out the necessary details of his plan: A visit to the doctor to get his prescription for sleeping pills renewed. His private affairs to be put in order. A time chosen when everyone would be out or safely occupied and not running loose about the house, Ilse would be the greatest danger of course, but he guessed wryly that if she knew he was to be out she would seize the opportunity to occupy herself with her lover.

So two days after his private catastrophe, he impudently 'borrowed' Linda's car.

He drove deeper into the country, away from the main roads, but not a great distance from Hawkswood for he would have to return on foot. He stopped in the shade of some elm trees, locked the car carefully, and walked away. He had no difficulty in entering the house unseen and climbing the long, turning staircase up to the attics in the roof, which no one visited now. He peeped into them one after another, mildewy, mouse-haunted chambers littered with trunks and gilt-framed oleographs with their winsome faces to the wall, and broken-down iron bedsteads. There was one attic, with a ceiling that sloped right down on one side to a funny little Victorian grate that seemed not unfriendly. With the unconsciously prim gesture of a landlady he touched the thin mattress, pressed down the springs: it would do.

The bed creaked under his weight as he sat on the edge of it, the ends of his tie dangling, his collar unfastened, swallowing pills. It was not easy to swallow them when his throat was so dry. When he had swallowed nine, he stopped. He took off his coat and folded it up to lay his head on. Then he unlaced his shoes and stretched himself out with a sigh. He wondered what the servant girl was like who had last used this bed. He tried conscientiously with his failing brain to imagine the round blank face and shallow light blue eyes . . . the black stockings . . . pink twill corsets stiff with bones . . .

*   *   *

Ilse could not but wonder uneasily why Werner had said nothing to her about the bedroom door locked in mid-afternoon. She had evolved a passable tale, but was too canny to offer it unmasked.

He did the following day, put into her care all their essential documents. 'If anything should happen to me . . . ' he had said; and she had replied: '*Bübchen*, don't be so absurd! What should happen to you?'

The formal handing over of the documents, the fragment of dialogue (with variations of course) had been performed before. Because she was sure they would be performed again, many times, she paid no attention. She had learned not to take Werner too seriously.

Still, when dinnertime came and he did not appear at table she did feel a slight agitation. He never went off without telling her. There was nowhere for him to go. She muttered that she hoped nothing had befallen him, and did exchange one panic-stricken glance with Ivor.

By eleven o'clock that night she had phoned the police. Because Werner had closed the garage doors behind him, they did not discover that the car was missing until the next morning.

After that, Ilse had no doubt.

She no longer imagined that he had been knocked down or met with some other kind of accident. It was only too plain to her that at last he had done as he so often threatened and killed himself — to punish her for being 'naughty,' because of course he had known all along the truth of that afternoon and had not wished to listen to her lies. In the

afternoon the police found the abandoned car and began a systematic search
of the countryside. At houses around
about, people were asked if he had been
seen.

Ilse looked ghastly.

It was Linda who found him. On some
ill-defined impulse of imagination she
went from room to room; and yet perhaps
if she had really thought to find him, she
would not have dared to look. He was in
almost the last room there remained to
enter. He had not even troubled to lock
the door. He lay on his side, on the dirty
striped ticking, his knee slightly drawn
up, his gray face on his bundled coat.

Linda dropped on her knees in the
doorway, afraid to go nearer, and rattled
off a hasty prayer for his soul. She was
desperately shocked. The mere fact that
he could kill himself horrified her; she did
not even pause to wonder why he had
done it.

But after that one flurried prayer she
banged to the door and hastened
downstairs to tell — whom should she
tell? She almost fell into Ivor's arms and

flooded into sudden tears as she said: 'He's *dead*, Ivor! Oh, he's *dead!*'

The first thing Ilse said when they told her was, self-betrayingly, 'Did he leave a message?' A letter to say why he had done it? It was a great relief to learn that he had not. She had not dared even to tell Ivor her fears. Now she began to cry with reaction, very pathetically. It brought a lump to Linda's throat.

It unbalanced Priscilla, too, in her adolescent romanticism. It had the effect on her of making her fanatically religious. She evolved for herself and adhered to a complicated arrangement of prayers and secret, absurd asceticisms. She was at that age. She determined to become a saint and save Werner's soul by the sanctity of her own life. For the first time in her young life she had expended on another person all the emotional force of her thwarted, badgered little heart. His death left her more desolate than the death of her father. There was a little shrine in her bedroom before which she lit candles every day, but 'The candles in the shrine of her heart never went out.' This beautiful sentiment never failed to bring tears to her eyes.

She wished Ilse liked her better. She would have loved to talk to her about Werner. But Ilse had no time for little girls. It was partly in the attempt to show her that she was not so childish that Priscilla took her Ivor's letter to Linda, when she found it in the corridor. (That too was a painful disillusionment. She had adored her Aunt Linda, seeing her as a Mrs. Do-as-you-would-be-done-by, all grace and sweetness, with love to spare even for an orphan. And then the letter . . . Priscilla had picked up the fluttering fold of paper and opened it to see what it was. The very first words told her everything . . . Her wrists trembled. Her face burned as if with fever. She was revolted and ashamed. She did not know how she was ever to face her aunt again. She did not know what to do with this hatefully betraying letter. She longed for the wisdom of Werner, and then she thought of Werner's relict, that woman of the world, Ilse; she would understand and she would know what to do.) But even then Ilse did not take her into her confidence. She merely advised her rather sternly that she had done quite right, and to think no more about it.

Behind Ilse's severely composed face lurked triumph and malicious delight. This was just what she needed to force Ivor's hand a little or, on the other hand, to persuade Linda into a more amenable frame of mind. She would not part with it for a thousand pounds. It could not be used just yet of course; it would be indecorous so soon after her husband's death to be thinking of such things. But in a few weeks . . .

It was a pity, from Ilse's point of view, that before she had time to use the letter, Linda died.

8

Edmund, juggling all the cold irons in his fire, found one after another dropped away. He was beginning to realize that he could not hope to hold Genevieve forever in this precarious manner. He must find some way to bind her to his side more securely. It was not so much that he feared to lose the delights of her person but all that she represented to him of dazzling wealth. It was all this that he longed to possess, with Genevieve the supreme titbit like the fairy at the top of the Christmas tree.

He really felt for Linda a murderous rage when he thought of it, not violent, but a steady fermenting bitterness like ichor in his veins.

He developed a queer habit, half fantasy, half earnest, of inventing elaborate plans for getting rid of someone who lay inconveniently in your path of life. He thought, *if this was a detective story now* . . . For he had heard that it was often the practice of detective novelists to work out their plots by imagining a method of ridding themselves of some real acquaintance they happened to dislike. So he used to sit hour after hour in a rigid trance at one of the writing desks in his club, a pen in his hand that never made a mark on the crested sheet of writing paper before him. He would think, *if I wanted to get rid of Linda in a story how would I set about it?* And of course the first thing of all would be to establish an alibi, because naturally the husband would be the first suspect. Yes, it would quickly be discovered that he had quarreled with his wife or was not living at home; then they would probably rake out that he had a mistress, a very desirably rich woman, and he in desperate need of money . . .

In the cheaper newspapers he began to study the accounts of fatal accidents. He made it a practice whenever possible to attend the inquests of these reported accidents and kept account of the verdicts, noting with particularity how many were recorded as 'Death by

Misadventure,' how many were 'Open Verdicts,' and how many received a graver decision. It was astonishing how many people died from a fall in a bathtub or down area steps on a dark night, and how many people went to sleep with the gas on, or drank out of the wrong bottle, or took the telephone into the bathroom to make a call while they lay in the bath: all things that could so easily happen to a person through someone else's dexterity.

Only, for that, you had to be present on the scene yourself. And then where was your alibi? No, he must have — that is, the hero of his book must have a method absolutely foolproof. The hero — or was he a villain? No, a hero, because he was not going to be discovered of course. Very well, then, the hero must lay the trap in such a manner that it sprang when he was not there. The difficulty there would be to make certain that it was sprung by the right victim.

He would prefer to meet her face to face and kill her openly; in some queer way, it seemed fairer. Or was it that he wanted her to see his hatred, he wanted to acknowledge his guilt to her?

The major snag in this plan was the disposal of the body. He knew how difficult that was and how often it had proved the undoing of many a hapless murderer.

It would be easy enough to get her to come for a drive in the car with him on one pretext or another; then the shot, or the blow on the head — but after? It had been daylight a moment ago while they drove through the Common, but now it was suddenly night and the car bumped in the dark over the tussocks, driving toward the quarry. (It would look as though she had fallen . . . Or in the river, her clothes swirling about her, her hair like weeds . . . or buried beneath the floor of a deserted house . . .) But he knew that although these places sounded so cunning and safe, it was only a delusion. After weeks or months the body would turn up and small dreadful signs would lead the police inexorably toward its destroyer. 'The Girl in the Quarry' discovered under all that limestone and bracken; he could see her broken face with the hair blinding it, and the wedding ring spinning on her finger bone . . . 'A Body in the River,' caught in the roots of the willow below the weir, a body of grotesque white coral with pearly eyeballs . . . Or 'Corpse in Cellar,' when they took up the rotted floorboards and found, on a bed of quicklime, teeth . . . and a silver watch with an inscription in the back . . .

Genevieve amused herself pretty well in London, all things considered, even though she was condemned to an oddly solitary sort of existence. At present it was still a glorious adventure. It was delicious not to feel the photographer's 'eye' ever on you, to let go one's highly trained social sense and be simply, deliciously oneself: a woman in love. She half believed it could last forever, just as it was, on these unreal terms.

Then that came to an abrupt stop.

For some days she had felt a little strangely, as if she were sickening for gastric flu, which was prevalent that September — not ill enough to want to see a doctor, not ill enough even to mention it to Edmund: just not her usual radiant health. She had an idea what the matter was, and it gave her thought. She would have to see a doctor, of course, there was no bucking that. She particularly did not want to ask Edmund for a doctor's name. It would be better for him to know nothing about it. And really all she need do was pick a name out of the telephone directory with a pin, the way people chose horses to bet on, if they knew no other way.

Then like a gentle beam of light illuminating her mind she recollected the comical drunk she had knocked down the first evening of her arrival. She had not given him a thought from that day to this, but she was glad enough to remember him now. He might not be very competent but he would do for a consultation of this nature, or if not he would recommend her to someone else. Dr. Paul, that was the name! She had noticed at the time that it was easy for her to remember because it was the name of her dead husband. Dr. Paul, somewhere in Harley Street, wasn't it?

She made an appointment for the following day.

He stood at the door of his glossy bower to greet her courteously as she entered.

'Mrs. Hamilton?'

'I see you don't remember me, Dr. Paul,' she said with a smile.

'Have we met before? It hardly seems possible that I could forget.'

'It shows you suffered no ill effects afterwards, for which I'm thankful. And now that I think of it, perhaps it is just as well you don't remember.'

He looked astonished. As well he might.

'Can you remember — nearly four months ago — one evening in June?' she began, and added wistfully, 'You were awfully sweet about it *then*. The fact is, I'd only just arrived and I wasn't accustomed to the left-hand drive — '

'You knocked me down!' he exclaimed, slapping his hand on the elaborately tooled leather blotter. 'Great Scott! Of course I remember, and charmed I am to renew your acquaintance . . . I seem to recollect that we spent the rest of the night — Oh, now it's all coming back; there was another man with you — '

'Much to your annoyance. You kept trying to get rid of him — '

'Yes, I behaved shockingly — '

179

'Don't say that! You proposed to me very nicely.'

'Good heavens!' he said, laughing. 'And did you accept me?'

'I told you my affections were already engaged, but you were very sweet about it.'

'Well, well, well,' he said, 'well, well! I see I am to congratulate you, Mrs. Hamilton. I hope you'll be very happy,' he said rather more formally, because after all this was in consulting hours and not a social occasion, and in half-hour consultation he could not afford to waste time in chit-chat, however delightful.

She looked at him a bit askance, saw his eye rest on her wedding ring, and realized that because she had given her name as Mrs. Hamilton he had jumped to the conclusion that she had recently married the man she had been with that night. It was hardly the moment to disabuse him of the notion, so she quietly said:

'It's about that I've come to see you, Doctor.' And proceeded to describe her symptoms.

He became serious and attentive, looking very handsome and wise, with his pen in his hand jotting down notes from time to time and asking questions. He smiled at her, leaning back in his chair.

'Well, there doesn't seem to be much doubt about it, Mrs. Hamilton. I shall have to examine you of course. We shall want to assure ourselves that everything is going to be quite straightforward. Unfortunately, I haven't the time today, but you could make another appointment with my secretary, or if you prefer it I will visit you at home.'

'I've always hoped to have a child someday. I'm rather glad, I think.' She spoke dreamily, more to herself than to him. 'I hope — I hope it's going to be all right.'

'Why, of course it is, Mrs. Hamilton. You don't want to worry about anything. I'll look in on Wednesday, the day after tomorrow, just to set your mind at rest. Just carry on your normal life and try not to think of it as anything unusual.'

'All right, Doctor,' Genevieve nodded, with a wide, dazzled, inattentive smile. She was occupied with her thoughts, wondering with a sharp little pang at the heart whether it would be a small scowling freckled boy with reddish hair falling untidily into his eyes.

She was never one to make quick decisions, and she decided not to tell Edmund yet. She wanted to plan a little for herself first. She had a notion that the time had come for her to take matters into her own hands. Women always settled these things better without the interference of men.

The day following her visit to the doctor she did nothing, except pace through the flat and ponder. To arrive at a decision took much explicit thought, and her brain always felt to herself both cumbersome and shallow, so that to beat thoughts out of it and capture them was something of a painful task. She wished that she had a powerful mind, a logical and philosophical mind that would tell her all she wanted to know. As it was, she laboriously decided on the only course of action that seemed reasonably open to her, since she could never quite grasp more than one side of a question.

The next morning she dressed with great attention: a pale gray suit and a maize-colored silk shirt and a hat of two gray wings skewered to her head with a pin ending in a great knob of topaz that was a gift from Edmund. She deliberately wore no jewelry. She looked a little pale but extremely lovely. Even Alice, the acolyte at the dressing table, said with shy reverence: 'Oooh, madam, you do look lovely!'

At the back of the block was a lock-up garage where she kept the Packard. She drove it away southwards and arrived at Hawkswood about noon. Three children wandered up. The taller boy stood a little away from the others, frowning absorbedly at the car. The little girl came hopping like a robin to within a yard and then stopped. Genevieve shut off the engine.

'Hallo!' she said invitingly.

They said Hallo gravely.

'I bet I know who you are,' Genevieve said, smiling at Jane.

Jane flushed crimson with embarrassment at this attention, attempted to run away backwards, tripped, and sat down bang on the lowest step.

'You're Jane, aren't you?'

'She's Jane and I'm Oliver,' said the little boy, running filthy little fingers, like pink fronds delicately uncurling, lovingly over the chromium trimmings.

'I wonder if you could find your mother for me. Could you?'

'I expect so,' said Jane not budging. And then suddenly she ran away down the path toward a young woman with a basket, and clasped her round the thighs. She must have said something, for the young woman looked up and quickened her step. Their governess, perhaps, thought Genevieve, seeing the girlishly simple cotton frock, the untidy wind-blown black hair, the bare legs thrust into muddy brogues, and wondered if even today a governess could allow herself to look so ungroomed and set her pupils such a bad example.

The girl came up with an uncertain smile.

'Did you want to see me?'

'I wanted to see Mrs. Campion,' said Genevieve in her pretty gentle voice. 'Would you tell her that Mrs. Hamilton would like to see her?'

A singular expression came into the girl's eyes.

'I am Mrs. Campion,' she said.

'Why, I'm so sorry. I don't know how I came to make such a stupid mistake,' said Genevieve, with a smile that Linda took for malice.

'Janey, would you carry this very carefully into the kitchen and tell Mrs. Hacker the carrots are for dinner and will she please scrape them.' She handed her the basket. 'Don't forget to say 'please,' Jane. Will you come in?' she said to Genevieve, preceding her up the steps. She opened a painted double door leading into an enormous shadowy room. 'We never use the drawing room nowadays, so no one is likely to disturb us here . . . '

She herself perched watchfully on the arm of a chair, opposite but rather frigidly distant. She was wretchedly conscious, in face of the elegant creature opposite, of her unkempt hair, her hands dirty from vegetable picking, her muddy shoes. It wasn't fair! She should have had the chance to make herself presentable. She was seized with an unreasonable fury, and thought, how dare she come here!

'I guess you know who I am,' Genevieve began. She hesitated. 'I wonder if you wanted to see me as much as I wanted to see you. I thought if we could only meet and discuss the whole situation through rationally, without letting our emotions get involved in it, we might get to a solution. It isn't fair to any of us to go on as we are, is it?'

Linda said nothing.

Genevieve said in a low voice: 'I can see you blame me for having fallen in love with Edmund. But, you know, it's a thing that can happen to anybody. You're young and healthy; do you imagine you'll never fall in love again in your life?'

'I know that people do fall in love with people they shouldn't, even after they're married; but if such a thing happened to me, I wouldn't give in to it, I'd be ashamed. I wouldn't pretend it was something honorable and all right and inevitable and make that an excuse to leave my husband and children. I wouldn't leave all my responsibilities just to gratify my own lust, I can tell you. As if it was something to be proud of. As if it wasn't a sin.'

'A sin!' echoed Genevieve puzzled. 'Why do you call it a sin?'

Linda flung back her hair with a dry little laugh.

'Because adultery is a sin. Didn't you know? Haven't you ever heard of the seventh commandment and, of Him who said that to break one was to break them all, and even to look on a person with desire in the heart was the same as committing the act of adultery?'

'But my poor child,' Genevieve protested incredulously, 'you can't use that old stuff as a rule for life! Nobody could! Nobody in their right minds would attempt such a thing!'

Linda stared.

'But that's — that's blasphemy,' she whispered.

Genevieve suddenly felt as if her backbone had been taken away from her; she wanted to cry; and for the first time understood what Edmund meant when he said that arguing with Linda was like trying to explain something to a particularly dense foreigner who didn't understand a word of your language. It had been a mistake to come. They had no common basis of understanding.

A fly buzzed and banged up and down the window.

She gave Linda a sad little smile.

'It's hopeless, isn't it? We just don't understand each other.'

'I'm sorry,' said Linda sulkily, as if she were being reproved for stubbornness by her teacher. She looked down at her hands in her lap. 'I don't know what you expect me to do.'

'That's simple,' she said. She made a little impulsive gesture with her gloved hands. 'I came to ask you to divorce Edmund.'

Linda said sternly:

'Surely he's told you I shall never do that.'

'I thought — if you knew I was going to have a baby . . . you might change your mind.'

Linda gazed at her stolidly, though her face had lost color.

'Why do you imagine I should care?'

Genevieve said quietly: 'I've never had a child. I'm thirty-two. And I'd like to have Edmund's child, more than I can say. But of course I couldn't have it unless it was going to be legitimate, that wouldn't be fair. It rests with you.'

'I don't think I understand. What is it to do with me?'

'If you will divorce Edmund so that he can marry me, there's no reason why I shouldn't keep the baby. But if you won't, then I shall have to get rid of it.'

'That's *murder*,' said Linda breathlessly.

Genevieve went to her, took her rough little hands in hers.

'Please, Mrs. Campion,' she pleaded. 'Don't be so hard on Edmund! Try to understand. You're young! I know what a splendid person you are really. With all that you've had to bear, you couldn't be otherwise than an utterly integrated personality. Can't we try to be adult about this thing? After all, maternity is a woman's natural function, isn't it? Won't you let me have my baby?'

Linda snatched her hands away and put them behind her back like a schoolgirl. Her face was red and defiant, her eyes scared.

'And what about my baby?' she said.

'Your baby?'

'Isn't he to have a father?' Linda asked almost pertly.

Genevieve stared at Linda for what seemed an eternity, searching those blue frightened eyes, dropping in shamefaced suspicion to her gaunt little frame in its faded blue frock. It became very difficult to stand because her legs were trembling. She said:

'Are you going to have a baby?'

Linda nodded.

'Didn't Edmund tell you?' she asked ingenuously.

Genevieve went deathly white.

She said through stiff lips: 'Then he knows?'

'Of course.'

Genevieve muttered: 'I'm sorry . . . could you get me a little water?'

She sank down in a chair and struggled with the agonizing little hat that seemed to be gripping her forehead in a vise. Finally she remembered the pin and withdrew it. She pulled off the hat with a sigh of relief and pressed her trembling hand against her damp brow. She lay there in a kind of black trance till Linda loomed through it with a glass of water. Linda opened the windows and a blessed little air wandered across the room. The fly that had been buzzing against the pane dived headlong into the sunshine. Genevieve took greedy sips of the not-quite-cold water. She thought, *That was my poor baby making me feel like that*; at three months the heart begins to beat; and a tear ran unexpectedly down her cheek. She said aloud:

'I'm sorry to have behaved like that. I'm all right now.' She sat up and powdered her nose, and sleeked out her damp hair with a comb.

Linda said: 'I don't want to hurry you away. Please sit there till you feel all right. But I have to go and see about the dinner, if you'll excuse me.'

'No, I'm all right,' said Genevieve, getting to her feet. 'Don't go yet, Mrs. Campion! I want to say — ' She came toward her with an expression of deep truth in her face. 'I want to tell you that it's going to be all right. I'm going away. I shan't see Edmund again. I mean it,' she said and turned away, unable to bear the

191

expression on Linda's face. She groped about blindly for her bag, her gloves, her hat, and with a little smile pinned crookedly to her lips said goodbye to Linda and walked away.

Linda stood there with parted lips and head flung back, listening to the car gliding over the gravel with the sound of rain. Then she closed the door and fell on her knees. She crossed herself and folded her hands. Her lips moved. Her eyes were closed, her upturned face looked like a blind woman's, rapt, groping, incommunicable.

When she had finished her prayer, she got up with a peaceful face and began straightening the room, fastened the window, pulled-to the shades, stretched the dust covers over the chairs again.

She felt something under her hand as she tucked the sides down and, lifting the sheet, she took out from the chair arm a fine silver hatpin with a great jewel on the end like a smoky yellow diamond.

She recognized it for the ornament that Mrs. Hamilton had worn in her hat. She looked at it discomfited. It was doubtless very valuable, and what on earth was she to do with it? She muffled the sharp point of the pin in her hankie and thrust it into her pocket for the time being.

Her mind was in such a turmoil as she served the dinner that she hardly knew what she was doing. Ivor, who had been tapping away boringly at his typewriter all morning, said to her as he passed:

'What's the matter? You're white as a sheet and your eyes are like jewels! What's happened?'

'Wait for me in the drawing room,' she commanded.

'The drawing room? What kind of a prank is this?'

'We shan't be interrupted. Please, Ivor? Don't argue!'

Priscilla saw them whispering in the shadows and looked quickly away for fear of what she might see next. She thought she would die if she should see them embrace.

Linda did embrace Ivor, but not just then; later, when she ran into the drawing room, she flung her arms about him and hugged him ecstatically. Ivor was so taken aback by this totally unexpected caress that he could not even respond to it. It did flash wildly through his mind that perhaps at last she was offering herself to him, but he did not find the notion entirely credible.

'Ivor, I'm so excited!'

'I can tell,' he said dryly. 'If I didn't know I should think you'd been drinking. Kissing me of your own accord! Wonders will never cease!'

'It's because I'm so happy, darling.'

'Thank you. I didn't imagine you had suddenly fallen a victim to my charms.'

'Who do you think came to see me this morning?'

'I'm not going to guess, so you might as well tell me.'

'Edmund's fancy lady . . . You may well look amazed. She came to beg me to divorce Edmund . . . because she's going to have a baby. What do you think of that?'

'What did you say? No; of course.'

'No; of course,' Linda agreed. 'I was very pious about it. Well, I mean, I did think it was disgusting of her to come flaunting her adultery with my husband to my face. Served her jolly well right, I thought, if she was going to have a baby. Though of course she'll get rid of it. She told me she would.' Linda drummed her heels on the floor. 'I do wish you'd been here, Ivor. I made her crawl. It was lovely. Then I told her I was going to have a baby, too. I told her I was seven weeks gone.' Linda fell into wild mirth, pressing her fist against her teeth to stifle the sound. 'You should have seen her face! Oh Lord! I thought she was going to faint. Then she said it was all over and she was going away and would never see Edmund again.' Linda clapped her feet in the air. 'And she meant it, she meant it. Isn't it wonderful?'

'Wonderful? You little fool!'

'Now he'll come back to me, don't you see? Do be glad for my sake, darling!'

Ivor leaned over her, his face dark and furious.

'You blithering young idiot, don't you see what you've done?' He shook her thin shoulders. 'Stop laughing, for Christ's sake, as if you'd done something clever.'

She sat up, pouting. She wiped the tears of unwise laughter from her eyes, and rubbed her shoulder.

'You hurt me, you brute! Why are you so cross with me! Men are weird!'

'Can't you see what you've done? Haven't you any sense at all? You've put yourself right in the soup, you bloody little fool. What did you want to go and tell her you were having a baby for? She may have believed it was Edmund's, but Edmund will know damn well it's not, won't he?' He continued with slow emphasis, 'And when she tells him why she isn't going to see him anymore, don't you think he's going to wonder where you got hold of this baby you were bragging about to his 'fancy lady,' as you so vulgarly call her? Doesn't it occur to you that this is the very opportunity he's been waiting for? If you've been unfaithful to him, *he* has no religious scruples to prevent *him* divorcing *you*. And, by God, he will! You've played right into his hands, given him the very information he's been praying for.'

Linda looked scared to death.

She crouched back in a corner of the sofa and whimpered, her hand plucking at her throat, her frightened, uncomprehending eyes fixed on Ivor's narrow sneering face.

'I shall tell him I was lying,' she said.

Ivor said dispassionately: 'My poor child that will hardly endear you to him, will it?'

. . . So Linda was thankful to be able to creep up to her room with her headache, after all. For the first time she found herself able to observe her own situation from the outside, as it were. And she saw it in all its hopelessness. She had been a fool ever to imagine she could win Edmund back. That sort of thing only happened in magazines and library romances, not in real life. Edmund wanted to be rid of her. He really wanted to be rid of her. At any price. She saw it all quite clearly now.

Ivor was right; she had been a stupid little fool; but life wasn't fair. Edmund would never forgive this trick. She knew him; implacable, vengeful, without compunction. She had given him the opportunity he was waiting for. She gave a little sob of self-pity. She wondered, with a dull petrified curiosity, what he would do. Escape! That was what she longed for! She wanted to escape from all her actions, from her fears and loneliness, from him, from them all . . .

For a long while she sobbed drearily into the pillow, tears that did nothing to dispel the ache at her heart. Then she sat up, fumbling in her pocket for a handkerchief. She stared, with a curious expression, at the hatpin lying on her hand among its folds. She blew her nose and dried her wet cheeks. The fingers of one hand explored gently the region beneath her breast where the ache in her heart seemed like a physical pain. In the triple mirror on her dressing table she could see herself seated on the edge of the bed, her dark hair tumbled on her dropping shoulders, the picture of woe. She exchanged a glance with herself, knowingly, pityingly. A great blob of tears spilled out and ran down her wan cheeks. From time to time she brushed them away with the back of her hand.

At last she sank back on the pillows and put the medallion she wore round her neck against her lips. On the wall opposite, the infant Jesus leaned forward to take her in his arms. With an odd little grimace of despair Linda suddenly drove the hatpin just under her breast, into the cage where her heart plunged like a terrified bird. Her left hand spasmodically caught the little medallion. Her face contorted as at a vision of terror. And then she lay still on the crumpled coverlet . . .

9

Genevieve really meant it when she told Linda she would never see Edmund again. The knowledge that Linda was going to have a child by Edmund, and that her pregnancy was the more recent by some five weeks, filled her with a horror that was insupportable. It was a betrayal of the coarsest, most animal kind. That Edmund all this while had been 'carrying on' with his own wife and deceiving his mistress struck her as the basest of lewd treacheries. He had sworn that there had been no intimacy between himself and his wife since he had known Genevieve, and that had been the biggest lie of all. It was more than likely a lie, too, that he had ever asked his wife for a divorce.

Now Genevieve's one thought was to get away — anywhere, so long as she need never see him again. She thanked God now that she had not told him she was *enceinte*. A wave of revulsion and self-pity swept over her, and she feared that seeing him might weaken her will. She knew only too painfully how his touch could turn her limbs to water. But this time she was determined to carry out her resolve. Above all things she dreaded a scene. She wanted to slip away without farewell. If her luck held it would not be as impossible as it sounded. Edmund was gorging at a business luncheon in the City and was not likely to be back before three . . . And that reminded her that she must be sure to get to the bank before then so as to provide herself with sufficient money. She hadn't the vaguest idea where she was going, but that was the least of her problems.

It was nearly two when she drew up in Brook Street and, leaving the car outside the entrance, hurried upstairs, her mind full of details. There would be various small bills and she must remember to send a covering check to the agent.

She was calling for Alice before she had got her key out of the door. Then she slammed the bolts home and locked it

— just in case Edmund came before she had left. She would not let him in; he could think what he liked.

'Alice, we're leaving,' she announced, pulling off her hat and gloves and flinging them on the bed. 'Get out all the trunks. Everything. I've got just about an hour to get out of this place, so we'll have to make it snappy. I'll help you to pack.'

Alice, dragging in trunks and suitcases, ventured:

'Where's madam going?'

'I don't know, Alice. You can send any mail that comes to my bank. It's just that I have to leave right away, and I'd rather you didn't know where I was going because then, if anybody asks you, you won't have to lie when you say you don't know.'

Since all the doors in the flat were open to facilitate their constant passage to and fro, she instantly heard the sounds she was half waiting for: the terrible quiet sound of the key grating in the lock. She went as white as the slip she held in her hand. She looked at Alice in terror and put her finger to her lips. She had to strain to hear through the thudding of her heart.

The key twisted . . . then silence . . . then, cutting the silence like a sword, the bell. Mechanically folding the slip, she stuffed it into a case, her eyes on the front door. The bell rang twice more. He assaulted the door with his fists: 'Genevieve!'

'Genevieve!' the door shook in its frame. 'I know you're in because the car's outside . . . Genevieve!'

Then there was no sound for so long that she began to relax. All her muscles seemed to ache with their effort of stillness. To avoid the maid's eye, she stooped and picked up a yellow check sports jacket and tried to push it into an overfull grip. It was while she was on her knees before the case that a faint sound in the bathroom caught her attention. She paused, trying to identify it . . . She looked up, on instinct and saw him standing in the doorway. She almost screamed. She sprang to her feet in a spasm of unreasoning terror, clasping an antique silver mirror defensively to her bosom.

He regarded the disheveled apartment

expressionlessly. He could not imagine what had happened. But why lock the door against him? Why look so startled?

'Apparently no one ever dusts a fire escape,' he said, surveying his hands. He stepped into the room. 'Going away?' he asked.

'Yes.'

Alice was on her knees slipping shoes into worn-out stockings with the blank and deaf expression of the correct servant; but she heard Edmund ask laconically: 'Bad news?' and her mistress answer: 'I know everything.'

'What is it that you know, may one ask?'

Her eyes met his accusingly for an instant. She said shakily: 'I'm never going to see you again.'

Edmund said: 'All right, Alice. You can cut along now.'

She looked askance at her mistress and then 'cut along'.

Genevieve said: 'I've been to Hawkswood and I know everything. I never want to see you again.'

'Just like that? You were going to run

away and leave me without a word, without giving me a chance to explain?'

Her knees would scarcely support her.

'I don't want to hear any explanations. I don't want to talk about it. Please go, Edmund.'

'Damned if I do, till I know what it's all about.'

She said with bitter clarity: 'I have seen your wife and I know she is going to have a baby.'

He looked at her uncertainly and then began to laugh.

'You don't mean to say you believed her. You might have known she was lying. That is, if she pretended it was mine . . . Come, you don't mean you were going to walk out on me just for a fairy tale like that? Oh, my dear, where's your sense of proportion?'

'Please don't make a scene, Edmund,' she begged.

'I'm not making you a scene. I'm simply trying to understand how you can be so crazy as to fall into Linda's trap and do the very thing she wants you to do. Just because she tells you some fudged-up tale about having a baby you go right off the deep end. It isn't reasonable.'

'It wasn't a tale.'

'Well, if she's having a baby, it's not mine, I can assure you of that. My God, how can you believe it could be when you must know perfectly well that we've meant nothing to one another for years? Can't you see it's a deliberate trick of hers to separate us?' He stared at her obstinate shut face in despair. He fell silent, thinking in a savage fury of frustration, *I'll kill Linda for this, I swear before God I'll kill her for this*. His feelings toward her just then were utterly merciless, that she should have maliciously succeeded in tricking him out of Genevieve. That he must not lose Genevieve was his one reiterating thought: that he could *not* afford to lose her and all that she represented to him of wealth and happiness and security: it was as if he said, *I will accept life on these terms and no other*.

He stood with his back to her, watching her in the dressing-table mirror as she moved to and fro. He kept picking up the bottles and lotions littering its top and pretending to be absorbed in them to hide his sick desperation. For a long time he stood there with a bottle in his hand staring at the label. He must have read it twenty or thirty times without the words reaching his mind. It was called SEDI-DORM . . . his eye wandered incuriously over the Table of Constituents: chloral hydrate 20 grs . . . potassium bromide 30 gr . . . extract of hyoscyamus 5 mins . . . syrup 2 dr . . . water 1½ ozs . . . To be taken on retiring. He did not remember her ever taking a sleeping draught; she must have brought this with her from the States, probably to take on the boat. Soon she would be on the boat again, if he could not prevent her. *If he could not prevent her.* The blood rushed into his face so hotly that he broke into a sudden sweat. He slipped the bottle in his pocket.

'Lord, I want a drink,' he said. 'Do you mind?'

'Alice will get you one. Ring the bell,' she said indifferently.

But he had already opened the door and seen Alice's tail disappearing through the opposite door as he did so. He went into the dining room and poured out two stiffish whiskies. 'Alice!' he called. 'Where's the soda?'

When she brought the fresh siphon, he said, squirting a little into each glass, 'You'd be sorry to lose your mistress, wouldn't you?'

'Yes, sir,' said Alice noncommittally.

'Then you'll be glad to hear that she's not leaving, after all. A little misunderstanding, Alice,' he said cheerfully. 'You run off and enjoy yourself for the rest of the day. We shan't need you again,' he added, slyly tucking a note in her palm and folding the fingers over it with a fatherly pat.

'What about dinner, sir?'

'We shall be out.'

'Thank you, sir,' said Alice without enthusiasm, and went.

'I thought you could probably do with one, too,' said Edmund, in the bedroom, handing Genevieve her drink.

'No, thanks,' she said stiffly, not looking at him.

'Come on, it'll buck you up! Can't we have one last drink together — as if we were parting friends?'

208

She took the glass, in silence.

He wanted her to meet his eyes, but when he raised her chin she drew sharply away. She shivered.

'Don't touch me. Please.'

He looked at her ironically.

'Sit down for a few moments. I won't come near you, I promise, if you can't withstand me.'

She flushed and her eyes filled with tears. Quickly, she swallowed half the liquid.

'Do you really mean to go?' he asked, with a whimsical look. 'Would nothing persuade you to change your mind?'

'There's no use talking about it, Edmund. Will you ring for Alice? I want to get on with my packing.'

He came closer.

'Alice is out.'

'Out?' she echoed in alarm.

'I sent her away.'

She put her hand to her face. She said vaguely, 'Why?'

'Because I want to hold you in my arms just once more,' he said huskily with his cheek against hers. 'Darling,' he whispered, kissing her throat, 'darling!' He picked her up in his arms, and she tried to push him away with a dignified gesture, but her hands only feebly pawed the air. She felt deliciously helpless, drunk. He fastened his teeth gently on her laughing lip, and she gave a little animal cry of pleasure as she felt herself sinking on to the bed, sinking down with him into darkness . . . into sleep . . .

He looked down on her as she lay there, with a queer considering expression on his face. He tucked a pillow more comfortably under her cheek and covered her with a spread.

'Sleep sound, my pretty,' he said softly.

He 'borrowed' the Packard and drove down to Hawkswood, leaving the car on the Common and taking the short cut through the copse up to the house. The ladder someone had left leaning against the upper windows gave him an idea. He drew on a pair of brown kid gloves and pulled a shabby tweed cap low over his eyes. He slipped in at the side entrance into the cloakroom and locked the door. In the glory hole under the stairs he found a battered box of tools and took out a screwdriver, a piece of wire, and a pair of pliers. It was while he was looking for his old battle-dress, that he wore for cleaning the car when he was at home and kept in the glory hole for convenience, that he came across something else — a child's grotesque mask in stiffened calico, a merry bucolic face with chubby red cheeks, a smiling mouth, and sightless eyes of cobalt blue with pierced pupils for the wearer to see out of. He slipped it on and replaced his cap. Then he climbed into the khaki suit and put the tools in a pocket.

You would have thought to see him run up the ladder with a rag in one hand that he must be a window cleaner, even when he stepped over the window sill, inside.

It is one thing to arrange for a person to be electrocuted accidentally next time they turn on their bedside lamp; it is something very different to walk into their bedroom and find them already dead . . . murdered . . . by someone else.

It gave Edmund a ghastly 'turn' to see that jewel in Linda's breast like a malevolent yellow eye winking in the late

211

ray of sun. His instinct was immediate flight, but the sight of that jewel arrested him. As if he could fail to recognize it! Had he not given it to Genevieve himself?

With an uprush of terror he recollected her unreasoning haste to get away. If he had not returned in time she would have left without seeing him again, without a word of explanation. Now all that seemed inexplicable in her behavior was explained. To steady himself, he lit a cigarette. There was so little time in which to eradicate all traces of the crime and Genevieve's presence. He rubbed his handkerchief hastily over any polished surfaces she might be supposed to have touched, and stubbed out his cigarette in the ashtray.

With his gloved hands he removed the hatpin from Linda's heart. It was as he had hoped: there was no blood externally. As he carried her in his arms out of the room he was momentarily startled by a glimpse of himself in the mirror: the lifeless bonhomie of his expression combined with the crude pink and white coloring made an effect that was terrifyingly sinister.

Linda's fist, grasping the silver chain

she wore round her neck, caught on the newel post, and the weight of her falling body dragged her arm free. She lay in a huddled heap in the shadow where the foot of the stairs curve round. So might she have fallen accidentally if she had leaned over the balustrade too far.

The sound of children laughing floated up to Edmund as he ran nimbly down the ladder. A lady's bicycle leaned against the garage and he grabbed it. It was of course much too small; he was obliged to balance on it like an organ grinder's monkey. Behind him a voice cried out joyously: '*Daddy!*'

Involuntarily he looked over his shoulder.

He saw Jane's face break into circles of terror before she began to scream . . . The sound pursued him down the drive . . .

As Edmund drove into Brook Street he glanced up automatically at the top flat, *and went cold*. It was dusk and the windows he expected to see as dim blanks were blazing with warm gold. That could only mean Genevieve was awake — which was *unthinkable*. She should have remained asleep for about eight hours; he had been depending on her to provide him with an unconscious alibi, since she would never know that he had left her side.

He parked the car in the side turning and scrambled out of his battledress, chucking it with the mask behind the back seat. Caution advised him against using the front entrance, because even if Genevieve were awake, this was no moment to be seen and perhaps remembered — for Genevieve's sake as much as for his own. The bathroom window was still open, just as he had left it a few hours earlier. As he stood in the twilit bedroom, the door open a crack, he could hear voices, murmuring . . . In a little while they grew louder as they came into the hall. He heard an unfamiliar male voice say, 'I'm sorry to have missed your husband. I should like to have congratulated him. Ask him to look me up; I'd like to have a word with him.'

He heard Genevieve murmur in her rich drawl, and then a little laugh. 'Ha-ha-ha!' echoed the man, and then briskly made his farewells, and the door slammed behind him.

When Genevieve pushed open the bedroom door and saw him standing there, dark, motionless, tall as a spectre in the half light, she gave a small scream and flung out her hand to the switch.

'How you frightened me!' she cried. 'I didn't know it was you. For a moment, I thought — ' She shook her head and, with something of an effort, said: 'What are you doing here, Edmund?'

'Who was that?'

'That was Dr. Paul. Edmund; why have you come back? Where have you been?'

'Who's Dr. Paul?'

'Oh!' she said impatiently. 'The man I knocked down in Hyde Park that first evening. Surely you haven't forgotten.'

'What did he want?'

'To see me,' she said lightly.

'Too bad you opened the door . . . You ask me where I've been. To Hawkswood.' He paused significantly. 'I saw Linda.'

'Oh, Edmund,' she said wearily. 'I don't want to hear any more about that. It no longer concerns me. Can't you understand?'

'But this does, doesn't it?' he said, balancing the pin on his gloved palm. 'You didn't want to leave it behind you, surely.'

'Why; no,' she said, taking it in her hands. 'You gave it to me. I didn't know I'd left it there. Where did you find it?'

'Where you left it, I presume: in Linda's heart.'

But the words didn't touch her brain. She felt so queer and sad, and now this reminder of Edmund and their sweet love brought tears pricking to her eyes, and to conceal them she bent her head and pretended to be absorbed in polishing the rusty-looking shaft with her finger.

'Look,' she said, showing him the brown mark on her pink skin. 'What is it?'

He said laconically: 'Blood.'

This time she did hear and with a startled face cried:

'*Blood!* But how horrible!' and let it fall, so that it rolled off her lap and across the carpet. As she scrubbed at her finger, the other words belatedly reached her brain, and she asked with uneasiness:

'What did you mean just now, Edmund

— 'in Linda's heart'?'

'It was in Linda's heart. The blood on the pin is her blood. Are you trying to tell me you didn't know she was dead?' he said with sardonic incredulity.

'*I* know! How should I know?' But there was terror in her face. 'How can she be dead? Is this some macabre joke? I won't believe you.'

'If you didn't kill her, why the desperate hurry to get away?'

'*If I didn't kill her!*' Genevieve repeated in a sort of hoarse treble like a boy's breaking voice. 'Why on earth should I kill her? Are you out of your mind?'

'So that I should be free to marry you, perhaps?' Edmund added thoughtfully. 'I imagine that would be what the Prosecution would suggest.'

She wanted to say, *Why should anyone think I want to marry you?* Then the recollection of the child she carried supplied the terrible answer. Through the dark mist enveloping her, she heard Edmund say:

'That was why I removed the pin. If no one saw you come or go, you ought to be safe enough . . . The real danger now is that damned Dr. Paul of yours. Pity you answered the door.'

Dully she heard herself ask why.

'He may become a rope round our necks, that's all.'

'A rope round our necks,' she echoed through her fingers. 'What does that mean?'

'They hang you for murder in this country . . . Come!' he said sharply. 'Don't lose your nerve, for God's sake! Pull yourself together . . . I only meant that his coming ruined the perfectly good alibi I'd carefully prepared.'

It took her a little while to work that one out. She had a shamed recollection of submitting to his embrace and then falling into this heavy slumber . . .

She said sternly: 'You arranged it. You gave me something to make me sleep, didn't you . . . ? So that I shouldn't know you'd gone away. You thought I'd still be sleeping when you got back and you'd be able to crawl in beside me and pretend you'd been there all the time.'

She stared at him with her hands over her mouth.

'Why do you look at me like that?'

'You killed her,' she whispered. 'I see. It was a plot. You killed her with my pin. Who but you would choose that particular pin — the one you knew was mine because you had given it to me yourself.'

'You're hysterical. Why should I want to incriminate you? And I didn't kill her, I assure you; and if I had, it would not have been like that. Besides, I brought the pin back, so where's the incrimination?'

'You had to show me what you'd done. You couldn't expect me to take your word for it without proof. That was all you wanted it for, as a hold over me, to keep me from leaving you.'

'Don't be a little fool!'

'Do you dare to deny it? Then what was this elaborate arrangement of an alibi for?'

He stared at her in silence and then said:

'It's no use beating about the bush. There isn't time. I've often wanted to kill Linda since I've known you and there seemed no other way out because she was so obstinate about divorce. I was so afraid of losing you today that I thought I would kill her. It didn't seem to me too high a price to pay for you. No, listen, I meant to kill her, but when I got there she was already dead.' He added in a low voice: 'I thought you must have done it. So I 'covered up' as well as I could. Tried to make it look like an accident. Please believe that's the truth. I know now I was mistaken; whoever killed her, it wasn't you ... That's all the 'plot' there was about it.'

She gave a strange dry little laugh.

'All! That was all the plot ... just to use me as a screen to protect your own precious skin. I was to be dragged into a horrible scandal. I was to be innocently involved in a hideous murder trial. I was to perjure myself. I was to be exposed to ridicule and scorn as 'the other woman.' My private life was to be dragged through the mud, subjected to every ruthless glare of publicity, from my personal belongings to my most sacred beliefs, for every dirty-minded man and woman to gloat over. And that, you say, was all! ... And to think that if it had not been for Dr. Paul I should have known nothing about it . . . *How could you!* How could you do this to *me*, whom you are supposed to *love!'* She was trembling all over with the violence of her heart's thundering. She still had a queer dazed feeling that this was happening in a dream, it seemed too vivid, too dreadful for real life; it was like no reality she had ever known. With shaking hands she struggled to fasten the straps on her cabin trunk.

Incredulously, with disgust in his voice, Edmund said: 'You'd let me hang! I do believe you'd let me hang sooner than have the world think badly of you. How very odd! I had no idea you were capable of such baseness.' He thought contemptuously, *She has the mind of a servant girl.* And it seemed to him that now he really did see through all her pretensions to the shallowness and commonplace vanity beneath. It was her illusory delicacy that had fooled him. She was nothing. Worthless. Stupid. Without substance. A beautiful but hollow shell played on by the wind. His first impression had been right, as first impressions always were; it was a wonder that he could have deluded himself for so long.

What was in his mind was not pretty.

He picked up the topaz pin in his handkerchief and weighed it pensively in his hand. Genevieve wondered if the shuddering contempt she felt for him showed on her face. Now she read meanness into his thin-lipped mouth and brutality into the pugnacious jaw. She remembered how repulsive she had found him before she fell in love with him. She wondered that she could ever have permitted those hands to touch her, that mouth to kiss her own; the mere thought of it turned her deadly sick now, and she imagined she must have been temporarily out of her mind that she could have fancied herself in love with him all this while. She felt for him now a passion of hatred as keen as her previous passion of desire. That she could ever have endured his embrace caused her a sickening self-contempt. There was a world of loathing in her eyes when they met his. They glared at one another like animals. It was as if scales had fallen from their eyes and each saw the other's soul naked and ugly, and they were ashamed.

He said with terrible cheerfulness, his lips pulled back in the semblance of a smile:

'Well, now we know where we are, don't we? It's simply a question of providing me with cover for those few hours when I was covering up your tracks — as I thought. I know it won't be easy to persuade you, but this — ' he held up the pin — 'may encourage you to cooperate. It's got a nice set of your fingerprints on it where you handled it just now, and a little of Linda's blood. The police would regard it as quite a trophy, wouldn't they?'

She said softly, intensely: 'I would rather hang, myself, than do anything to help you! Nothing you could threaten would make me lie for you. Nothing you could do would make me stay.'

'No?' he said. And smiled.

She imagined herself escaping . . . and his footsteps pounding after her down the stairs . . . those iron fingers catching her hair, pulling her back, and pressing the scream into her mouth again . . .

With a tremendous effort she made

herself say coolly and deliberately:

'Don't be so absurd! You can't keep me here against my will; I'm an American citizen.'

He laughed: perfectly genuine laughter.

It was that which frightened her into a panic, so that she tried to get past him to the door . . .

His arm was like a bar crushing her chest . . . She felt trapped, frantic, maddened with fear . . . striking with her sharp heels, digging her nails in like claws . . .

He cried: 'Ah! You vixen!' and struck her on the side of the head so hard that she staggered wildly, waving her arms, and tripped backwards over a valise lying in her path. Then she lost balance completely, and fell, cracking her head loudly on the ironbound corner of her cabin trunk.

'Oh God, you've killed me!' she cried. A look of alarm and vexation passed over her face. She groaned slightly once or twice, but she made no attempt to move.

When Edmund went across to her, he found it was as she said: he had killed her.

PART THREE

PART THREE

10

No one at the Rivoli Cinema, Howcester, remembered a patron answering to the description of Ivor Campion on the afternoon of Wednesday the 10th. No usherette had noticed a man with a limp. The girl at the pay desk did not recognize the dark face in the photograph. It was no go.

No one recollected him at Timothy White's either.

'But why should they remember me?' protested Ivor. 'I didn't even buy anything there. They didn't have what I wanted. It's a gadget for cleaning gutters, a sort of wire scoop for raking dead leaves and rubbish out of the tops of drainpipes. Maybe it wasn't Timothy White's even. How should I know? I just went into the first ironmongers I saw. What of it? Are you supposing I never went to How-cester?'

'No, Mr. Campion. We know you went.'

'The barber will remember. I go every week.'

'Yes, he does. You had an appointment for three o'clock, and you kept it.'

'Why all the fuss then?'

'You could have caught the three-thirty back to Hawkswood. You could still have killed Mrs. Campion at four, tipped her over the stairs in an attempt to make it look like an accident, and then made your official entrance, just after six.'

It took Ivor quite a few moments to regain his pose of studied nonchalance. He reminded himself that it was futile to get angry with their solemn stupidity. What did one expect of county police? He sneered back at them coolly.

'I've never heard such utter nonsense. In real life people never have proper alibis, you ought to know that. Actually, it's too absurd, because as it happens I was very fond of poor little Linda. I mean, mere opportunity isn't enough, you know,' he explained condescendingly. 'What you need is proof.'

'Oh, as for proof,' said Inspector Trevor patiently, 'we have plenty of that.' He began hunting through a sheaf of loose papers in his dossier.

It's curious how small a thing can unnerve one if the circumstances are just right. Ivor knew perfectly well that he had nothing to do with Linda's death (apart from a wretched twenty-four hours when her death was still thought to be 'accident,' and he had feared that perhaps she had deliberately hurled herself over the banister because of what he had said to her earlier); and yet Trevor's cool assurance that he had proof up his sleeve was enough to make Ivor panic, with a sense of guilt that was all the worse for not being reasonable.

'Ah,' said Inspector Trevor, withdrawing from the pile a small crumpled sheet, much scribbled over. 'This, for instance.'

From where he sat Ivor could recognize his own writing, and his heart began painfully to thud. 'You might like to have a look at it,' said Inspector Trevor, handing it across to him.

He read:

Just knowing you has altered my whole life, darling. That had been crossed out and underneath was written: *Linda, why don't you trust me? How can you believe I would do anything to harm you? Edmund's last words to me yesterday were —*

And again that last sentence had been scratched over. Similar sentences went running on down the page.

'Why, this is just scribble,' said Ivor. 'It doesn't mean a thing.'

'Not that side, Mr. Campion.'

He turned the page over. On that side too a letter had been begun and abandoned. It must have been fished out of the waste paper at some time. It was intended for Edmund, but he had changed his mind about sending it halfway through and never finished it.

Patience, patience, dear coz! You shall be rid of her. But it takes time. The rather elaborate preliminaries are now concluded. In a very short while, I judge, the fatal step will be taken — or I am not the man you take me for, or that I take myself for either.

Ivor said feebly:

'This was a joke of course. Not very

230

funny, I agree. But you can't really imagine that this indicates a plan to dispose of Edmund's poor wife. Is it likely I would have mentioned it on paper if there had been such a plan?'

'Some people do queer things,' said the inspector stolidly. 'Still, we should welcome an explanation. Perhaps you could make us see the joke.' He added with undisguised grimness: 'It seems serious enough to us.'

It was not a very pretty story that Ivor had to tell; but he was obliged to tell it. It began with running into Edmund in Bond Street, by chance, soon after the end of the war in Europe. They had a drink and a talk about old times, in the course of which Ivor was asked what he was doing, and he said, nothing. Edmund seemed preoccupied and restless, seemed scarcely to know why he was in London or how his family were. But the next time they met he was in quite a different mood and he wanted to talk about himself. He told Ivor frankly all his troubles: That he was ruined and would have to sell his home. That Linda was largely to blame.

That they had become wretchedly incompatible. That he wanted his freedom. That Linda refused to divorce him, though she knew he was in love with someone else. That it seemed the best thing he could do was to slip under a bus. That everything was hopeless, hopeless. His future was blacker than it had been at any time during the war. And the whole train of disaster hung from Linda's shoulders. If he were free to marry the woman he loved everything would be all right; she was very rich.

And Ivor asked idly: 'Can't you divorce her?'

Edmund said, By God, didn't he just wish he could. No grounds. She had never looked at another man. She wasn't that sort of girl.

Sergeant Drake was scribbling in the corner.

Ivor said rather sheepishly:

'I said, in the idiotic way one does: '*I'd* better have a go at her — Ivor the Irresistible.' I only meant it as a joke, because I used to have a terrific success with a certain type of woman. I'd only seen Linda once or twice, years ago, when she was just a pretty kid. I honestly meant nothing by it. But Edmund lighted up. He swore he'd give a hundred pounds to the man who could seduce her. He said if he could get evidence of adultery, he'd pay the co-respondent two hundred pounds. He asked me — and I suppose he was serious — whether he could hire a man to do the job. I laughed, and said I was broke to the wide myself. I offered to do it for two-fifty. To my amazement, he said: 'Done! How long will it take you?' I still half thought he must be joking. But he wasn't. If the husband was willing, it seemed priggish to back out. He came to fetch me the next day and took me down to Hawkswood. I was glad to go because I needed building up; not even a blind old maid would have looked at me as I was then. However, I meant to do my best to keep my part of the bargain, too. I thought it would amuse me. It was far tougher than anything I had imagined. Poor Linda was what is known as a good girl, and she happened to be in love with her husband. She could not be got to believe that he no longer loved her and would never love her again. Since she could never get him back, I hoped I might provide a little fun for her by way of compensation. It was very hard work, and slow work, and Edmund with creditors at his heels was naturally getting a bit impatient: Was I going to bring it off or not? This unfinished letter was to tell him that I thought I was.'

'And the letters you wrote to her were all just — '

'A part of the campaign. She was so — almost prudish, that I was obliged to pretend I was deeply in love with her, and even then the notion shocked her. Luckily, I mean luckily for me, she had a strong vein of jealousy in her; all women are dog-in-the-mangerish about letting another woman have something they don't want themselves, and I found I could quickly rouse her feelings if I feigned an undue interest in Mrs. Hauser's attraction.'

'Did you ever see the woman yourself?'

'Edmund's girl? No. Cagey old devil, trust him! All he told me was that she was an American and fabulously rich.'

'You don't know her name or where she was staying?'

'I know nothing more than I have told you.'

*   *   *

'It looks rather as if they've done a bunk together,' said Inspector Trevor to his sergeant, when the saturnine young gentleman had been dismissed. 'Or at least it would do if there was any way for him to leave this right little, tight little island. Unless he's managed to get himself some sort of job which permits him to leave these shores.'

It was as he replaced the slip of crumpled, scribbled-on paper in the file that his eye fell on Mrs. Potter's statement in which she mentioned that a lady had called on the morning of the 10th to see Mrs. Campion . . .

'I didn't see her meself,' said Nanny Potter, spreading her capacious lap. 'It was Lionel, I think, who mentioned it to me. Ever so excited he was about the car.'

Lionel remembered the car very well and described it enthusiastically. At school they collected cars. He had been awarded ten points for this one because it had an American number plate. Yes, he remembered the number plate, too. He had not had as much time to look it over as he would have liked because his sickening little kid sister had made a big show of herself and knocked their brother down, and he, Lionel, had been obliged to drag him away before they started a fight.

'Good boy!' commended Inspector Trevor, flicking a silver coin into the air. 'Jane, do *you* remember the lady who came in the big car?'

'She had a dear little birdie on her head. I wish she'd given it to me.'

'Was she pretty?'

'Yes, she was. She said: 'Hallo, Jane!''

'And what did you say?'

'I said, 'Hallo!''

'And then what happened?'

'Mummy came and tooken her away.'

'And you didn't see the lady again?'

Jane shook her head.

'Then the horrible man came.'

She leaned up against Nanny and hid her forehead on Nanny's hand.

Trevor picked up a child's A.B.C. and stared at the pictures absorbedly. He said, in an absent, lackadaisical sort of voice: 'What horrid man was that, I wonder?'

'A horrible soljer, he was, and he had a horrible face, and he comed down the ladder and he frightened me.'

'No, I don't know him.'

'I fort it was Daddy.'

Her plump cheeks whitened at the recollection and she began to tremble.

Nanny Potter said: 'There, there, my lamb! It was only a nasty dream. It didn't really happen. It was a nightmare she had, sir. I had nightmares like that when I was a little girl.'

It sounded like a nightmare but Trevor didn't think it was. If Priscilla had been there, she might have enlightened him. Still, Jane's mention of the ladder brought to mind the memory of her crying fit the evening her mother was killed, when she had flung herself down on the ground sooner than be dragged under the ladder.

That incident hardly bespoke nightmare. And it was true that the ladder did provide a convenient entrance or exit. Odd that he hadn't thought of it before.

★ ★ ★

At Edmund's club they had very little to tell the police. He was last seen there on Tuesday, when he had come in, collected his letters, and changed his clothes. He had been staying there intermittently for the last four months. He returned to the club to sleep most nights, coming in usually at a late hour and sleeping correspondingly late in the morning. He had left no instructions about forwarding his letters, nor had he given up his 'chambers.' There was a soldierly bareness about his room, few accoutrements, few clothes. Yet clearly he had not packed any. Why fly off without your clothes? That seemed almost as if his disappearance had been involuntary. There were no letters lying about, not a scrap of writing. Nothing in his pockets. No betraying addresses. No photographs. Nothing that gave any hint of personality. That was queer enough surely. And it seemed that unless he returned to collect his clothes, they had arrived at a dead end.

There was, then, nothing for it but to send out a description to all stations, asking for him to be detained for questioning.

They also inserted a piece in the daily papers.

11

Edmund was dazed with the shock of finding Genevieve dead. For a long time he knelt beside her stupidly, the ancient words 'She should have died hereafter' running round his mind, over and over, like a faulted disc.

She lay there clumsily with her head crooked against the trunk at an unconvincing angle. She did not look beautiful now. He did not feel sorry for her, he did not feel for her anything at all, he was only ponderously preoccupied with what he should do.

He ought to get away at once.

Only, as with Linda, he was the first person they would think of in connection with Genevieve's death. He must be known to visit her. No one had seen him come this evening, though. But the maid, who had heard them quarreling earlier, knew her mistress had suddenly decided to pack and leave.

Yes, that was it: she had packed and left, after all . . .

He got stiffly to his feet. His limbs ached with cold, as if he had been kneeling a long while in a marble chapel. He locked the door of the bedroom and went into the dining room and poured himself half a tumbler of neat brandy. It was then ten past nine and it took him nearly forty minutes to work out satisfactorily all the moves ahead. The only person who could spoil his plans was the girl, Alice. She would have to go.

He had to hunt around to find the things he wanted, the scissors, the sealing wax, the adhesive tape . . .

In the maid's room he found a brown trunk with the initials A.C. on the front in black. She had not many possessions fortunately. He was just scrutinizing a cheap navy linen button-through frock when she came in. She stood in the doorway, one hand on her hip, regarding him furiously.

'What do you think you're doing with my things?'

He looked up and said coolly:

'That's no way to speak to me.'

She went nearer and caught hold of the dress.

'Here, you give that to me,' she said indignantly.

He stared at her across the dress.

'You get out of my room,' she said. 'Go on! Hop it!' There was fear underlying the words.

'Alice, don't be such a silly girl!' he said; but she pulled her hand away and ran through the other rooms toward the bedroom.

She could see a line of light under the door, and she turned the handle; but the door was locked.

'Madam!' she cried, rapping wildly. 'Madam! ... Oh, madam, madam, madam, *madam!*'

She *really* could not be allowed to shriek like that, even though it was the top floor of an empty building. She died, what is fairly called, instantaneously. She lay heaped outside the door like an obedient dog.

Edmund burned the piece of string; the slow flame climbing illumined his face ominously from below. Then he unlocked the door and carried the dead girl into the bedroom. Then he went back to her room and fetched the brown trunk. That, too, was taken into the bedroom and the contents dumped on the floor. Only the navy linen dress with the white buttons down the front was put on one side. He began to undress Alice Cole . . .

It was five to eleven when he came out of the bedroom to knock back another stiff brandy. He was trembling with nerves and exhaustion, but the brandy encouraged him. The worst, he told himself, was now behind him. He tidied every room in the flat. Then he finished Genevieve's packing and locked the suit-cases. Her handbag had fallen between the wall and the bed and it was only the happy chance of pulling out the bed to unmake it that caused him to spot it. He pushed it into one of the valises. At last he carried the luggage downstairs and stowed it in the back of the car. The brown trunk with the black initials A.C. was locked in the boot.

One final look round the empty flat to

make sure nothing was forgotten, and then lights out and the door slammed.

It was then a quarter after midnight.

His idea was to put the luggage (except for Alice's trunk) into a depository, but naturally that could not be done for another ten or twelve hours. Till then he proposed to leave it in the Left-Luggage office at Victoria Station. After the luggage was deposited he meant to put the Packard into a garage to be 'laid up' for the winter months. By that time he might have found a discreet customer to buy it.

He drove right into the station. A yawny porter stacked the luggage on a truck and wheeled it away with Edmund following in its clattering wake. Because of the initials on Genevieve's baggage, he took out a receipt in the name of George Hallam. He tipped the sleepy porter and went back to the dark drive-in to collect the Packard.

Only to find it was no longer there.

That was a worse moment for Edmund than any he had yet had — worse even than the moment when he realized that Genevieve was dead. He damned nearly lost control of himself. His nerves were so raw that if anyone had spoken to him at that moment he would have screamed. He went on standing there idiotically because he did not know what to do next. Clearly he could not notify the police of the theft. He would just have to wait and lie low and see what happened. He covered his eyes . . .

★ ★ ★

The Packard was driven to a garage near the Embankment. They fitted it with new number plates, working fast. The man who had driven it in walked round and round it admiringly. He touched it with gloved fingers, testing various parts. When he found the boot was locked he opened it with a slender steel hook, more from idle curiosity than anything else. He slid the trunk forward.

'Here! A.C. Something for you to take home to the missus, Lefty. Same initials.'

Lefty stood up from where he was crouching to have a look. By the flare of the blowlamp in his left hand he saw gleaming a strand of yellow floss from the hinge of the trunk. Then he saw that it was hair. He thought, *human hair*.

He struck the locks two sharp blows with the point of the lamp and they jumped open.

'Go on,' he said. 'Push back the lid! You got gloves on.'

'Christ!' said the other, going green round the chops. 'It's a dead doll!' He slammed down the lid again in terror and shoved the trunk back into the boot. He stared at Lefty with white-rimmed eyes, 'It's hot, Lefty! What'll we do? The boss'll murder me for this, and I'm not to blame. Am I, Lefty? I couldn't know. Best thing I can do is to take the whole dump out and lose it, damn quick. I'll pick up something else.'

'Yer can't take it out with one plate on and one off. And the boss wants this job done for tomorrow. If it ain't ready, he'll raise Cain. You tell him what's happened. He'll have to know. Go on, you tell him.'

As Lefty had foreseen, the boss could not afford to lose the Packard now. The boss smiled. The boss said: 'Dispose of it;

got all night, ain't yer? Simple!' No need to panic; it was no business of theirs.

Soon after nine A.M. the Packard was driven out by a man who might have been a chauffeur in a dark suit and a peaked chauffeur's cap. At Westminster Bridge he drew up beside two quietly dressed men; one was small and scrawny with a hard red face like a groom; the other was also short, but thick-set, with alert eyes in a bloated olivine face. They didn't wait for the chauffeur to get out and open the door for them, or he didn't bother to do so; they were in the car almost before it had come to a standstill. The car slid away up Whitehall and swung left. None of the men spoke. They sat bolt stiff against the soft leather upholstery; only their eyes flicked warily from side to side.

It was still too early in the morning for the pavements in that very fashionable street to be crowded — as they would be in two hours' time. The Packard drew into the curb, its engine gently throbbing. The short thickset man got out, with quicker movements than you would have supposed from his appearance, and

247

slammed the door. From then on it was a matter of timing.

There were only two customers in the jeweler's shop and they were both women: one had brought in a watch to be mended and the other to collect her pearls after restringing. The thickset man asked to see diamond bracelets . . .

Inside the Packard the scrawny red-faced man who might have been a groom sat looking at his watch. Then he leaned forward and opened the door with his left hand; his right was in his pocket. The man who might have been a chauffeur muttered, 'Okay, Rats!' And Rats darted across the pavement and dived over the threshold of the jeweler's shop.

'Get together there!' he said sharply, motioning them with his gun. 'Bunch up! Bunch up!'

One of the women saw the gun in his hand and screamed. He drove his fist into her teeth casually, with a slow-seeming gesture, but with great effect.

The assistants' arms were upraised. They moved toward one another in shuffling obedience. Their eyes were furtive, startled. The gray-haired one flung himself on the alarm with the sublime élan of a Nijinsky — a movement that would have been impossible to him five minutes earlier. The jangle was deafening. But the thickset man still continued methodically stowing jewels into his open-jawed black bag for another fifteen seconds.

'For Christ's sake!' said Rats.

The thickset man turned to go. One of the assistants moved. And Rats fired, winging him. Outside, people were running up. The thickset man was on the pavement, in the car, and Rats was at his heels. 'Beat it, Jack!' he said, as they scrambled in. As the car sprang forward, a youth boldly leaped on the running board. Rats screwed down the window and just tapped him on the forehead with the butt of his revolver. His scream came faintly back to them as he fell away.

Two streets away a police car waited to intercept them. They rode out at the Packard, and to avoid it, the Packard without losing speed mounted the pavement, bumped a lamppost, swerved, and knocked down an old man.

As they tossed away over the curb they could see through the back window people gathering about the old man on the ground. They weren't picking him up.

The thickset man kept muttering: 'Faster! Faster, can't you!' but the driver did not bother to reply. They were going like hell already, through the traffic and jumping the lights, but the police kept close on their tail. At the Paddington wharfs they abandoned the car and separated, running between the warehouses, dodging for shelter among the high blank walls.

It was Stop Pressed in the noonday editions: *Bandits £20,000 jewel haul in daylight raid West End. Jeweler shot.*

The police had of course several unreliable eyewitness accounts of what the men looked like; but they also had the abandoned Packard, and they hoped to get quite a few ideas from that. It did not take them long to find out it was stolen; but it seemed to the divisional inspector highly curious that the theft had not been reported. So it was given some cunningly evasive publicity in the press in the hope that it would elicit some useful response.

Edmund saw it, which is hardly surprising since he was on the look-out for it. It was almost a relief to read that it had been found, the anxiety of waiting had been so great, though it could scarcely have been connected with worse circumstances. There was no mention of the trunk. He took that for a good sign. If they had found it there would certainly have been an outcry. Still, he must find somewhere safe to lie low.

He had gone from Victoria Station to the Piccadilly Palace Hotel, as a suitably busy place where visitors could arrive at any unreasonable hour without comment. He withdrew a couple of suitcases from the Left-Luggage to provide himself with a solid appearance; they were of no use to him of course, because they only contained Genevieve's clothes.

He arrived there in the early hours of Thursday morning (the same day as the raid), but it was not until Saturday morning that he connected it up with the stolen car that the paper was writing about at such length that morning. He realized that he must go to earth for a time. He had on him just enough cash to pay his bill at the hotel. He must not cash a check, they were too easy to trace. And then he recalled that he had pushed Genevieve's handbag into one of the suitcases — she always carried a lot of ready money on her. He scrabbled through it eagerly. There were nearly seven pounds. There was also a gold compact and cigarette case. A lot of other junk of course, such as all women carry . . .

Among the old letters was one un-posted one. It was addressed to Prescott & Kale, the estate agents. He remembered that she had heard from them on Monday, inquiring whether she wished to take up her option. She had written to say she would like to renew her lease for a further three months. She had told Edmund she had. And after all she had not sent it. *She had not sent it*, he repeated to himself, *and in a week or two the lease would run out*.

It was useless to send it now, because she would not be there to sign the agreement when it came. He shuddered. He had, then, perhaps a week, perhaps more, in which to make his getaway.

He had already had to do a little shopping: toothbrush, razor, clean shirts and socks; now he bought a secondhand raincoat and snap-brim hat and a pair of glasses with heavy dark rims. Having his hair darkened, too, made a difference. Bottled suntan obscured his freckles. He found a room of sorts in a dingy house in Delancey Street, Camden Town. It smelt abominably and the whole house was alive with curious sounds at night, but he felt safer, much safer.

He would have felt considerably less at ease if he had realized that the police had found his battledress and the calico mask, where he had bundled them behind the back seat of the Packard.

The battle-dress was put through the usual routine and was traced, rather disappointingly, to a Major Campion of a little village called Hawkswood Bottom in Kent. However, a man went down there, merely to tidy up that end of the affair. He naturally checked up with the local police before he went to Hawkswood house and was surprised to find that the inspector there rather thought they had got something.

'But we can't tell you where he is,' the inspector said. 'We should very much like to know ourselves.'

Mrs. Wragg, who owned the little newsagent's next door to The Condemned Man public house, identified the mask by her private mark still visible inside the cheap cotton 'form.' Old Mr. Marriot up at the house had bought the last (it being really a Christmas novelty line, and just one or two left over from last year's season) a few months ago for his grandson's birthday.

Inspector Trevor gingerly tried it on, and stared at himself in the mirror. He put on his hat and pulled the peak low over his brows, shading its fixed imbecile smile and horribly blank blue eyes.

No wonder the child had screamed. Not nice to think you saw your father, and then discover he had quite another face — a red grinning face like a ventriloquist's doll, fixed in a false leer.

Not nice at all.

12

Mr. Roderick of Prescott & Kale, the estate agents, naturally wrote to the tenant of the Brook Street flat before the lease ran out, to ask whether she wanted to renew. He was surprised not to receive an answer. The following day he tried three times to get her on the phone, and thereafter left instructions with the office girl to ring that number whenever their phone was disengaged until she got a reply. It is contrary to the agreement of furnished premises for them to be left unoccupied by the tenant without due notification to the agent or owner; there was always the risk, for instance, of pipes bursting, taps left running, electric fires not switched off and so on. It was this that worried little Mr. Roderick, not the rent, which had been paid in advance to the end of the quarter.

So he went around with his duplicate keys to exercise his right of entry. Being

255

an American she might not know the laws existing between tenant and landlord, she might not have read her lease attentively, and she might without thinking have gone away for a few days without telling the agent. He expected it to be something of the sort. He was thunderstruck to find she had apparently packed all her traps and left the place for good.

It was while, again in the apartment, he was checking the inventory that he saw the sealed cupboard in the bedroom; and what is more, Mr. Roderick did not remember it being sealed when he had taken the inventory in the first place. What was especially curious was that it was sealed with tape all the way round the edge. It took him quite a time to get it off. And then he had to find a key that would unlock the door (he had far too much regard for his clients' property to think of smashing the lock; but one cupboard door key is not unlike another.

When he got the cupboard open, the poor little gentleman fainted.

★ ★ ★

The papers called it: MYSTERY WOMAN FOUND DEAD IN WEST END FLAT. It read this way:

A dark-haired woman in her twenties was found in the sealed cupboard of a top-floor Brook Street flat by Walter Roderick, estate agent, who had gone there to see the tenant of the flat. He was astonished to find the tenant had apparently left and taken all her things with her; and it was while he was checking the inventory that he noticed the sealed cupboard. Mr. Roderick could not identify the dead woman, who was wearing a red silk dressing gown, but he affirmed that the dead woman was not Mrs. Hamilton, the tenant of the furnished apartment. Mrs. Hamilton he described as a blonde about thirty years old, and a citizen of the United States. The police are anxious to trace Mrs. Hamilton, as she may be able to identify the dead girl. The garage, where she kept her car, state that Mrs. Hamilton took it out Wednesday morning. She did not mention that she would not be bringing it back. The car, a 1942 café-au-lait Packard with a New York number plate, was noticed outside the building until a late hour Wednesday night. A man who is believed to have visited her was seen to drive away about seven P.M. that evening in a Daimler car.

And so on. There were in fact two mystery women. Because where was Mrs. Hamilton? Although that aspect was not stressed in the papers, the police, from Mr. Roderick's information, believed there was something decidedly queer about her disappearance. It was so sudden. It was considered highly probable that she could answer a great many questions about the dead girl: not only who she was and what she was doing in the cupboard, but why she was wearing an expensive dark red brocade housecoat over tattered rayon underwear and cheap walking shoes and lisle stockings. Her nails were painted, but her hands were the hands of a girl accustomed to rough work. The housecoat bore the label of a noted American house. There was a theory that she might have worked for Mrs. Hamilton as a maid, and when her mistress was out, put on, as maids will, her mistress's housecoat in which to make an impression on her boyfriend — and then something happened and she was killed. She had been strangled.

From there it was an easy link-up with the stolen Packard of the jewel robbery. So that meant that wherever Genevieve Hamilton had disappeared to, it was not in her car that she had gone.

But there of course they were mistaken.

Dr. Paul came forward and told the police that he had visited Mrs. Hamilton by appointment, professionally, in the flat in Brook Street and had left in his Daimler a little after seven. He described her. There appeared to be no one else in the flat; she opened the door to him herself, and herself fetched glasses and so forth when he accepted a sherry before he left. He said he had met the husband on a previous occasion (this was the first the police had heard of a husband; the flat was in her name; however, they encouraged the doctor to talk). 'They were only engaged when first I met them,' he said. 'Hamilton was a rather stocky, red-haired chap, as I remember, but I couldn't pretend to an accurate description.'

He laughed wryly; it had just occurred to him that they might not have been married, after all; she had an excellent reason for calling herself *Mrs.*

The man in the antique shop on the ground floor said the American woman *had* a boyfriend; he had seen him nearly every day, a rather pale-faced, soldierly looking man with leaf-brown hair and a surly expression. One or two of the girls from the Russian milliner's workrooms also remembered seeing him on the stairs sometimes.

So it was mentioned in the papers that the police wanted to see a red-haired man in connection with the disappearance of Genevieve Hamilton from the flat where the brunette was found murdered.

Actually they knew who the brunette was now, but they chose to keep the information to themselves for a little while. The milkman knew all about the dark-haired maid in the top flat. Alice Cole her name was. Came from The Midlands, Derby, or somewhere. He believed her parents lived there still. Father was a cobbler, he remembered that.

The police found her parents and she was officially identified. Once Inspector Trevor saw the significance of the anonymous khaki and the carnival mask, he handed over the Campion dossier to Scotland Yard. It was more than ever necessary to find Edmund Campion. That these curious articles were found in the Packard pointed to this being 'the fabulously rich American woman' he was reputed to be in love with. They had apparently disappeared together, that seemed plain enough; and if they were in a hurry to get away (and they certainly would be in a hurry if he had just killed his wife), that would account for them not daring to report the theft of the car in the normal way. It would be wiser to lose it and save themselves alive.

There were three separate fields of inquiry: The search for the jewel thieves, who had stolen the Packard or received it knowing it to be stolen, wanted also for robbery with assault, use of firearms, manslaughter, and, very possibly, the murder of the woman Cole. There was the search for Genevieve Hamilton, who had unaccountably disappeared. And there was the search for the missing husband of the dead Linda Campion. The photograph which used to stand on Linda's dressing table was printed off and circulated to all police stations. Even if Edmund had known this, it is doubtful whether it would have agitated him unduly. The photograph was six years old and he considered that his dark disguise radically altered his appearance.

All the same, he scarcely went out till nightfall. The papers alarmed him. He was horrified to learn that Alice Cole was found so quickly. He had reckoned on at least a month's security from that quarter. Bad luck seemed to dog him in this affair. He felt like a fly in a spider's web; the effort to free one limb entangled another more securely. It was horrible. And most terrifying of all to him was that no mention had been made of Alice Cole's trunk having been found in the boot of the Packard. He could not understand why the police should keep quiet about it if they had discovered it.

It did not escape repulsive old Mrs. Sailor's notice that the new lodger — George Hallam, as he called himself — was a devoted newspaper reader.

Edmund was perfectly aware of her inquisitive eye on him, but he rightly judged her to be suspicious by nature with a nosiness born of years of hard experience as a lodging-house keeper in a London slum. As he was naturally reticent it was not difficult for him to be secretive; he had no fear of giving anything away.

Nor would he have, if he had not seen two policemen on the doorstep as he leaned out of the window. One of them stepped back and looked up, as if to see whether it had stopped raining; and Edmund ducked quickly in again. He opened his door and, picking up his raincoat, tiptoed to the stairs. He heard Mrs. Sailor twang: 'Well, come in, then.' And then those ponderous boots. And the front door slamming.

Beyond that he dared not wait. He had

no time to lose. The fact is, he had lost his head, because he had the notion that policemen always went in pairs when they were going to make an arrest. He just took the time to lock his bedroom door, knowing that would hold them for a few minutes longer, and then he slid up the landing window and threw his leg over the sill. Below him a maze of grim washing hung on strings. He dropped onto the soot-black wall beyond which the goods trains shuttled purposelessly all day long. He slithered down onto the track, which rendered him liable to prosecution, and walked slowly in the direction of Mornington Crescent. He treated himself to a wash and brush-up at Dirty Dicks, thrown in for the price of a pint. The doors of the Gaumont were just opening. CONTINUOUS PERFORMANCE was written in colored glass letters across the porch. It was warm and dark inside, and he had such an embryonic longing for warmth and darkness. He pushed a shilling over the brass-topped desk and entered. He stayed there till ten-thirty that night chiding the notice of usherettes by the simple expedient of moving every now and again to different parts of the house.

He dared not wander the streets for fear of being picked up. He was afraid to go back to his lodgings. He found a doss in Bayham Street and paid in advance because he had no baggage. The bed was filthy and rats ran across the floor. He sat up all night. But at least he did not dream.

The policemen had called at the Delancey Street lodging house to check up on an alien who had tactlessly omitted to register his departure. Mrs. Sailor was a landlady who liked to keep on the right side of the police. 'A woman alone . . . ' she would begin morosely, inserting a finger between the greasy wool turban and the matted hair and having a good scratch.

She soon noticed the draft from the landing window and wondered who the devil had had the bloody sauce to open it. And what for, she immediately asked herself. With her life, she was not slow to jump to the obvious conclusion. She had seen the top-floor go out very bright and early; he had come down to the basement to tell her, as if his own virtue astounded him, that he was going straight to the labor exchange. Wasn't the whole performance a little over ostentatious? Might it not have been a ruse? And she rushed upstairs to see whether the top-floor had sneaked back to collect his things and clear. He had not. She came down more slowly and stooped to squint through Hallam's keyhole. The key was not in the lock; that meant he was not in the room.

She turned the handle gingerly.

No, he'd locked it as usual and gone out — only that meant he'd managed to get out without passing her in the hall. So the cops had put the wind up him! She'd summed him up all right. 'That's right, ducky!' she commended herself, and vigorously scratched her poll.

When he did not return all night, she considered herself quite within her rights as a respectable landlady to have a poke at his luggage. He'd left a bottle of suntan behind him in his flight, she noticed. Even poor old Sailors-don't-care, as her pals called her, knew enough to recognize the worth of the alligator case and the pigskin one. It was a pleasure for such a skilled workman as she was to pick their locks — it was one of the few things besides gin that she still enjoyed.

She gasped an obscenity at the sight of the furbelows within. Her filthy old hands lovingly stroked the satin, the chiffons clung to her roughened fingers. Oh, the *lustful* little nighties! Her imagination rioted squalidly. She went through everything methodically. Luckily for Mrs. Sailor's moral welfare, Genevieve's furs, Genevieve's jewels were in the big trunk; the suitcases held mainly underwear, shoes, and bags. All the same, it was only uneasiness about their source that prevented old Sailors-don't-care from secreting some of the things under her skirt before she went to the police. Because, as she said with plain logic, 'What's he doing with two cases full of women's clothes, and not even a collar of his own?'

The police also found the question interesting. More so, when they had examined the contents of the suitcases carefully and seen that nearly everything in them was of American make. Larceny, housebreaking, burglary, all forms of theft and robbery were such a commonplace to the Camden Town division of the Metropolitan police that they did not at once connect the initials G.H. on the bags with Genevieve Hamilton, the missing American woman. They then inquired about Mrs. Sailor's lodger, late-departed. She told her story with practiced fluency, her eye, like an oyster in its rough gray shell, peering out at them ginnily, coldly. She identified cautiously the photograph they showed her. 'Could be, on'y he looks darker. Dyed, I daresay,' and she mentioned the suntan on the mantelpiece.

The police net spread. All lodging houses in the district were notified.

. . . Edmund left Bayham Street after that one ghastly night. His money was getting very low. His mind was beginning to go over the edge: he imagined he heard people calling after him in the dark street; the little pasty-faced girls, so like mildewed cinquecento angels, in the feebly illumined bakers' shops where he bought buns, seemed to stare at him with a special knowledge;

or if he stayed in his room, the downstairs wireless seeping through the floor kept muttering: 'Edmund Campion . . . Wanted for Murder . . . Last seen . . . '

The landlady of the Belmont Road room, in Chalk Farm, wanted to see his Identity Card. She said it was a new order, watching him primly between her lowered lids. For a moment he stood on the stairs, one hand in his bosom, like Napoleon; then he remembered and said wearily that it must be at the station with his luggage.

Hour after hour he sat upstairs hunched in his raincoat, deadly cold but lacking a shilling for the gas fire. He stared wryly at the oleograph of 'The Stag at Bay,' till it grew too dark to see; but all the time he was listening. And presently he heard the front door quietly close. He felt sure that she suspected him; yes, she had gone to the police.

In a fever of impatience to be out of the house, he hurried down stairs . . .

The landlady had gone to the police, guiltily, miserably enough; but no one wants to be murdered in their beds.

He scurried from them this way and that through the dark slippery streets. They caught him finally among the warehouses in Kentish Town. The sound of the police whistles was like knives piercing him. He stumbled. There were torches everywhere, shining right in his eyes. Someone, not near him, recited monotonously: ' . . . Campion, alias George Hallam, alias Hill . . . a warrant to arrest you for the murder of Linda Campion . . . '

He missed the bit about *anything you say being taken down and used in evidence* because of his laughter. It was less hysteria than sheer relief. Because he hadn't killed Linda; so what was there to worry about?

★　★　★

The day Edmund Campion was hanged for the murder of his wife, the body of an unknown woman was found in an Emergency Water Supply tank that was being removed to make a site for pre-fabs. The body was in a trunk so rotted with

270

the action of the water that it broke away as it moved. After some careful reconstruction the letters A.C. were just discernible on the front.

The dead woman had sustained a blow on the back of the head which had fractured her skull and also snapped the vertebrae at the base of the neck. She had good teeth, was a little above medium height, and fair-haired. She wore a platinum wedding ring, inscribed P. H. to G. S., 1932. That would make her between thirty and forty years old. Dressed at the time of her death in a navy rayon-linen dress with white buttons down the front, crêpe de chine underwear, American nylon stockings, and no shoes. She was in the third month of pregnancy.

The Campion Case being closed, there was no reason to connect her with it. She never was identified. Just one more nameless victim to swell the statistics of pregnant women found murdered every year in London (that sort of murder speaks for itself). If she could have had her choice she would have preferred it to be like that, anyway. She would not have cared to have that thing identified as the beautiful Genevieve Hamilton: she was always so particular about her appearance.

We do hope that you have enjoyed reading this large print book.

Did you know that all of our titles are available for purchase?

We publish a wide range of high quality large print books including:
**Romances, Mysteries, Classics
General Fiction
Non Fiction and Westerns**

Special interest titles available in large print are:
**The Little Oxford Dictionary
Music Book, Song Book
Hymn Book, Service Book**

Also available from us courtesy of Oxford University Press:
**Young Readers' Dictionary
(large print edition)
Young Readers' Thesaurus
(large print edition)**

For further information or a free brochure, please contact us at:
**Ulverscroft Large Print Books Ltd.,
The Green, Bradgate Road, Anstey,
Leicester, LE7 7FU, England.
Tel:** (00 44) **0116 236 4325
Fax:** (00 44) **0116 234 0205**

MOUNTAIN GOLD

Denis Hughes

Rex Brandon, internationally famous geologist, is flying to join a party of prospectors camped overlooking the frozen surface of Great Bear Lake in northern Canada, when his plane is forced down in a storm. Suddenly Brandon faces a 200-mile trek across the frozen wastes. Of the people he meets on his journey — all of whom want to get to Great Bear — several are destined to die, and Brandon cannot be certain that the survivors are who they say they are, or what their true motives may be . . .